Miss Ellie stood before the Ewing family, gathering her strength. "This is not going to be easy for me," she began. "I love you all very much, and I cherish Southfork. But now that things have changed, I have to do what my conscience tells me is fair and right. It pains me, but I feel I have no choice. I've decided to give Southfork back to my brother Garrison."

———————

Series Story Editor **Mary Ann Cooper** is America's foremost soap opera expert. She writes the nationally syndicated column *Speaking of Soaps*, is a major contributor to leading soap opera magazines, and is a radio and television personality.

Writers **Paul Mantell** and **Avery Hart** are, between them, the authors of plays, children's records, educational cassettes, and humor articles. They live in New York City but have come to think of Dallas as their second home.

Dear Friend,

Pioneer Communications Network takes great pride in presenting the eighth book in the Soaps & Serials paperback series. If this is your first Soaps & Serials book, you're in for a pleasant surprise. All our books give you a glimpse into the past, featuring some of the most exciting and entertaining events in the history of television soaps. For those of you who are old friends of the Soaps & Serials line, thanks for your support.

Now, here's a question we received from one of our thoughtful and loyal fans. A reader from Abilene, Texas, wanted to know if a visitor to the city of Dallas can tour the set of the television show and, if so, how can she get tickets? Sad to report that visitors are almost never allowed on the set of television shows in production. Also, Dallas is shot mostly in Los Angeles on the MGM lot. There is some location filming in Dallas, however.

Although we can't answer all the letters we receive, we still enjoy hearing from you. Keep writing!

For Soaps & Serials books,

Mary Ann Cooper

Mary Ann Cooper

P.S. If you missed previous volumes of Soaps & Serials books and can't find them in your local book source, please see the order form inserted in this book.

DALLAS™

8

THIS CHERISHED LAND

From the television series created by David Jacobs

Soaps™ & Serials

PIONEER COMMUNICATIONS NETWORK, INC.

This Cherished Land

From the television series DALLAS,™ created by David
Jacobs. This book is based on scripts written by Arthur
Bernard Lewis and Leonard Katzman.

DALLAS™ paperback novels are published and
distributed by Pioneer Communications Network, Inc.

SOAPS & SERIALS™ is a trademark of Pioneer
Communications Network, Inc.

ISBN: 0-916217-88-4

Printed in Canada

10 9 8 7 6 5 4 3 2 1

THIS
CHERISHED
LAND

Chapter One

The bright sun shone over Southfork ranch, as it did most days of the year. At this time of the morning, the land had not yet heated up, and the morning breeze carried the scents of tumbleweed and mesquite. Cattle lowed and milled around in the distance.

Life appeared to be back to normal in the Ewing family, but everyone was still jittery over Bobby's kidnapping and the bloody rescue. In fact, Bobby was still staying home from work. It wasn't that he was afraid to get back into the swing of things, but he knew that his mother and father had been terrified out of their wits. To give their frayed nerves time to heal, he had agreed to help around the ranch for a few days, in spite of his impatience to return to his new construction business.

The rear door of the mansion banged open, and a small group emerged, their voices raised in various levels of frustration and annoyance.

First to appear out onto the patio was Lucy, the baby of the family, raised by her grandparents almost since birth. They had spoiled her, which was only natural, and now, at eighteen, she was showing the effects of a pampered life. Her age and background both made her impatient to be out on her own, and so she was doubly furious about the family's refusal to buy her a car so she could at least drive herself to and from school. And now, since Bobby's ordeal, Jock Ewing didn't even want to let his granddaughter attend school, much less drive there herself.

Trying to solve the problem, Pam good-naturedly volunteered to chauffeur Lucy while on her way to work at The Store.

The younger generation had been trying to convince Jock that the danger was over, but he was a stubborn old man and not easily moved. His immensely strong personality had helped him to become one of the richest and most powerful men in Dallas by the time he retired. Tanned and leathery now from working on the ranch, it was hard to picture him in a suit behind a desk in an office. But Jock Ewing was as at home in one as he had been in the other. Fortunately, his oldest son, J.R., was taking good care of the company. That is, as far as anybody knew. J.R. always played his cards so close to the vest that nobody ever knew much about what was going on, aside from the very impressive quarterly balance sheets.

"Will you stop wringing your hands, Daddy?" Bobby said. "Everything's all right now."

"Yeah," echoed Lucy. "I'll have my body-guard with me the whole way," she joked, gesturing to Pam.

"Kidnapping is no laughing matter, Lucy," her grandfather scolded her. "Your grandmother is still worried sick. Have a little consideration for her."

The other three looked at each other knowingly. How typical of Jock not to admit to his own fears, to insist that it was Miss Ellie who was to blame for his caution. They all smiled, touched by the old man's love for his family.

Pam put her arm around his shoulder. "Don't worry about Miss Ellie," she said, her tongue ever so slightly in her cheek. "I'll take care of her."

Without waiting for him to reply, Pam and Lucy hopped into Pam's car.

"Well, all right, then," Jock said gruffly, belatedly giving his permission. He turned with a shrug and strode authoritatively over to the breakfast table, where Raoul poured him his morning coffee—black and strong, the way he liked it.

Bobby walked around to the far side of the car to kiss his wife good-bye.

"Going to work today, honey?" she asked him.

He shook his head. "Daddy wants me to make a few phone calls for him today. Says he's busy with the roundup. . . ." He rolled his eyes as if to say "You know what that means."

Lucy shifted impatiently. Not that she cared about being late for school, but she was anxious to be off and on her own for a few hours, away from the suffocating grip of her family.

Bobby and Pam, noticing her annoyance, hurriedly kissed each other good-bye. "I'll have supper on the stove when you get back," Bobby joked.

Pam smiled, musing how odd it was that she was going off to work, while Bobby stayed at home. What a long way they had come since they'd been married!

In a large suite on a high floor of one of Dallas's most expensive hotels, a man stood looking out into the distance through the large, smoked plate-glass windows that reached from floor to ceiling. His face was worn and haggard, tired from a lifetime of struggle, and yet there was still a lot of the old vigor in it. He was tanned from years of being outdoors, and strong from hard work in the broiling sun and the driving rain. He was a big man, tall and broad-shouldered, with a salt-and-pepper beard that framed his round, open, masculine face.

Behind him came a knocking at the door of the suite, startling him out of his reverie. Lately, his thoughts and memories had somehow seemed so much more real to him than the so-called "real world."

"Cathy," he called, so that she could hear him in the bathroom. "Someone's knocking! Answer it, would you please?"

"I've got it," the woman shot back as she burst out of the bathroom and headed for the door.

He retreated back into the depths of the suite, not wanting to see anybody. He patted her affectionately as they passed each other. Cathy Baker was a hell of a good-looking woman, and a good person, too. He was grateful to have found her, deeply grateful.

The young woman strode to the door, trim, attractive and professional, in spite of the fact that she was dressed in next to nothing, having just come out of the shower. Before opening the door, she grabbed a robe that was lying handily on the sofa and wrapped it around her.

She opened the door to find the bellhop standing there, carrying a large, flat package. For a moment, he just gaped at the beautiful woman, so alluringly dressed, standing in front of him, before he came to and made himself to hand over the package.

However, she did not take it. "Would you mind putting it down over there?" she asked, pointing to the coffee table by the couch. "I'm all wet, and I don't want to get water all over it." Quickly, she tipped the boy and ushered him out. "Garrison, you can come out now," she called.

He emerged from the bedroom slowly, making sure that the boy had gone. In the last few months he had had no desire to see anyone —anyone but Cathy.

"Ah, it's the painting!" he said, rubbing his hands together avidly. "Well, get a scissors, and let's open her up!"

Cathy had meanwhile grabbed a towel and

was drying herself off, and now she went to the kitchen area to find the scissors.

Garrison picked up the package and mounted it on a chair so that they could look at it properly. Cathy returned with the scissors, and together they cut and stripped the brown paper wrapping. They stood there for a moment, taking it in.

It was a painting of a house—an old-fashioned, modest ranch house, painted white but in need of a new coat. In the background on the left stood a weather tower with a wind propeller on top. A few white clouds, the fair weather kind, hovered above the house, and trees surrounded it, providing some shade. It was an unexceptional painting of an unexceptional scene, but from the expression on Garrison's face it was obvious that the painting meant a lot to him.

It was equally obvious that he did not like it. As he stared at the canvas, his face grew beet red with anger. "Is this what they call a painting around here?" he exploded. "This looks like a page from a comic book! Why the hell did I think it would be better to get it done in Dallas? Just think of all the real artists in London and Paris who would have been happy to do it! Damn!"

Cathy put her hand on Garrison's shoulder to calm him down. She seemed to have the magic touch; the old man's anger melted as quickly as it had come.

"Garrison, does it really matter in the end?" she asked softly. "A painting is a painting, right?"

Garrison sagged down onto the couch, his anger completely spent. "You're right as usual, Cathy," he admitted. "I keep losing my temper, and not even realizing it . . . just like you said would happen . . ." His voice trailed off enigmatically.

The beautiful young woman looked at him tenderly, compassionately. Turning toward the painting again, she thought that it was not really bad at all, considering the artist had had only an old snapshot to work from. She mentioned as much to Garrison, and he laughed, calm as a kitten now.

"You know something, girl," he said, tousling her hair, "you're an amazing person, but what you know about art couldn't fill a thimble!" He was silent for a moment, his eyes shifting cannily, trying to put one over on Cathy and on himself. "Well, put the wrapping back on and have it taken over to Ellie Ewing, Southfork Ranch."

Cathy clucked her tongue at him. "Oh, all right, dammit . . . I guess I have to bring it there in person. I don't know why I promise you anything. You never forget a word I say!" She kissed him on the forehead and set to work wrapping the painting.

Jock Ewing remained on the patio for quite a while, drinking cup after cup of coffee, something Miss Ellie would never have allowed him to do, and reading his newspaper. He liked to keep up with the doings around Dallas from his easy chair, so to speak.

He was still there when the white pickup truck pulled up into the driveway and Ray Krebbs, the ranch foreman, got out. "Howdy, Ray, what's doing?" Jock rose to greet him as he approached. But he could see from the look on Ray's face that something was up.

"I don't exactly know, sir," said the foreman. "But someone just told me something mighty odd, and I thought I'd better tell you about it right away."

Jock put down his paper and gave his full attention to Ray.

"This guy, Ernie, he's one of the hands, and we were talkin' a while ago, and he mentioned that he was out by Section 40 two weeks ago, near that capped oil well, and he thought he saw a truck."

"So?" Jock asked, not understanding what it was Ray was getting at.

"Well, sir, you see, it wasn't one of ours."

Jock frowned. Something did indeed seem to be up, and he didn't like it. "How come it took two weeks for me to hear about this, Ray?" he asked, a little annoyed.

"Well, Ernie, you see—he heard yesterday about those cattle rustlers over at the Curl Ranch, and he started wondering."

Jock took Ray's arm and pulled him back toward the truck. "Come on, Ray," he growled. "We're gonna check this thing out right now."

Miss Ellie would normally have joined her husband for morning coffee, but with her daughter-in-law Sue Ellen pregnant, she was busy making preparations to welcome her second grandchild.

After breakfast, she and Sue Ellen had gone upstairs, and Miss Ellie had taken her into a room which had, until then, been one of the many guest rooms.

"This," she said, spreading out her hands to indicate the room, "is my idea of a perfect nursery!" She beamed at her daughter-in-law, who in turn looked pleased.

Then Sue Ellen frowned slightly. "But Miss Ellie—what if he cries during the night? Won't it wake you up, this being so close to your bedroom and all?"

But Miss Ellie brushed her off. The thought of getting up in the middle of the night to cuddle and soothe a crying baby sounded like heaven to her. It had been so long since she had cradled her own.

Sue Ellen looked around the room and saw a golden future in front of her eyes. No matter how badly J.R. had treated her, frequently stepping out with other women, now that she was carrying the Ewing heir, she had the whip hand, and she intended to play it to the hilt. Now J.R. would be forced to toe the line. She would be the queen mother of Southfork someday, and her son would be the future king.

A boy . . . she wondered why she had thought that with such assurance. After all, the baby might just as easily turn out to be a girl. But no, J.R. would never tolerate a child of his turning out to be anything but a boy, and J.R. had a way of getting what he wanted.

"It's gonna be a boy, Miss Ellie, I just know it," she said in spite of herself. Fearing for the way J.R. would treat a daughter, she dearly hoped that it would be a boy.

"A shy boy, if he's anything like his father used to be," Miss Ellie said softly.

Sue Ellen turned away from her mother-in-law, pretending to study the future nursery, but really to hide the deep blush that was covering her face. Miss Ellie must never know that the child's real father was, in all probability, not J.R. at all, but rather his bitterest rival, Cliff Barnes. And yet, she could not suppress a wry smile. It was such ironic justice, after the way J.R. had treated her all these years, giving her no love at all and saving it all up for his floozies. She had gotten him back but good and was enjoying being on top for a change.

"Oh, I don't know, Miss Ellie . . . I think this baby might just turn out to be a real extrovert —outgoing and friendly!" She thought of Cliff and smiled warmly.

J.R. had entered in time to hear this last remark. "What's up, you two?" he asked, surprised to see them together in the guest room when there weren't any guests. He was tying his tie and wearing his best dress suit.

His mother turned to him, clasping her hands in happiness. "Look around you, J.R. — this room is going to be your son's nursery!"

"Oh. That right?" he replied, uninterested. Picking out nurseries was women's work as far as he was concerned, and he had no patience for such stuff.

"Sue Ellen was just saying that you're probably going to have an outgoing, friendly son!"

"Well!" J.R. laughed good-heartedly. "What do you know about that! Just like his daddy, huh?"

Sue Ellen again looked away, this time to hide the sarcastic smile that crossed her face. "Exactly, J.R. Just like his daddy."

The note of irony did not escape J.R. Ewing. Very little did. He knew that his wife had been having an affair, and that the child was, perhaps, not his at all. Yet he also knew that, for the moment, he had no choice but to go along as if nothing were wrong. He couldn't risk Sue Ellen leaving him now, not when she was carrying what he hoped was the first Ewing grandson. His whole life he had lived to please his papa, and Jock had been waiting for a grandson for seven years, ever since he and Sue Ellen had been married. He couldn't let his daddy down now. Besides, it would be too humiliating.

"Hmm," he muttered, looking at his watch. "Well, I'm gonna be late if I don't scurry out of here."

Miss Ellie, so immersed in her own happiness that she had missed the spiteful gibes exchanged between Sue Ellen and J.R., turned to her eldest son and smiled. "Sue Ellen and I are just about to go into town and shop for bassinets and things. We could meet you someplace for lunch. Would you like that?"

For once, J.R. did not have to make excuses to get out of spending time with his wife. "Sorry, Momma," he said without hesitation. "I've got a speaking engagement this morning, and it's got a luncheon attached to it—seems the Jaycees want me to tell 'em what it is that made me such a success." He smiled brightly, satisfied with himself. He kissed both women lightly on the cheek and turned to go. Miss Ellie and Sue Ellen said good-bye and wished him a good day.

When he was gone, they turned their attention back to each other once again. "I don't know, Miss Ellie," Sue Ellen commented, "he doesn't seem very shy to me. . . ."

Ellie winked at her daughter-in-law and patted her tummy, which was just beginning to swell, but not noticeably so. "Not anymore, that's for sure," she said wryly, and started out of the room.

Sue Ellen stood there, rooted to the spot with shock. "Why, Miss Ellie!" She blushed deeply. "The things you say sometimes!"

For a former Southern belle, her mother-in-law was certainly full of surprises!

Bobby sat in the den, a stack of reports piled high on the desk in front of him. Beside him, in a bin, were some half dozen architect's drawings in cardboard tubes. Bobby held the phone in one hand and some papers in the other, but the business he was conducting concerned the ranch, not his construction company. Jock had handed him the rather mundane task of making some calls for the Grain and Feed Association on the pretext that Bobby was good at talking to "good old boys" and would get the job done better than Jock, with his oilman's abrasive manner. So here

Bobby was, phone in hand, talking about the Food and Drug Administration's new proposals concerning the use of antibiotics for cattle. But Bobby was never one to shrink from a job, whether he had chosen it or not, and he was involved in a hard sell when the doorbell rang. Thinking that Raoul would answer it, as he usually did, Bobby didn't think twice about getting up until, thirty seconds or so later, the bell rang again, more insistently this time.

Bobby was a little annoyed with Raoul, but the timing was what got to him. He shouted for Raoul to answer the door, but when it rang for yet a third time, Bobby resigned himself to the fact that Raoul simply wasn't around, told his caller he'd get back to him later, and went to answer the door himself.

He opened it to an unlikely sight. There in the doorway was an old man, large and bearded, and on his arm was a beautiful young woman. In his other hand, the old man held a package, a large package, and by the look on his face Bobby could tell that he was not a little uncomfortable. The woman was looking at her companion, as if to offer encouragement.

"Can I help you?" Bobby asked politely.

The old man looked at his lady friend, as if to a prompter, and then, turning back to Bobby, said, "I'm looking for Mrs. Ewing." He was looking at Bobby very strangely, as if he knew him, or should have known him.

"Well, sir, there happen to be three Mrs. Ewings that live here, and not one of them is home. Who exactly did you have in mind?"

The old man licked his lips, and his lady friend gripped him hard by the arm. "Ellie Ewing," he whispered.

"Well, like I said, she's out—gone into town for a few hours." Bobby fell silent; the man's intense stare and tight-lipped manner stifled conversation. Finally Bobby managed to remember his natural courtesy and asked the pair if they wanted to come inside and wait, or if there was anything he could do for them in the meanwhile.

"What time will Ellie be coming back?" the old man wanted to know.

"Well, I really can't say, sir," Bobby replied. "Sometime this afternoon, anyhow."

The old man seemed to have heard as much as he could stand to hear. Thrusting the package into Bobby's hands, he instructed him to give it to Ellie.

Bobby took the package, a little wary at the strange behavior of this visitor, and then, after a moment, found the voice to say, "Um . . . who shall I say it's from?"

"From a man she used to know many years ago, tell her," came the answer.

The stranger was staring at Bobby in that funny way again, making him very uncomfortable now. What did this fellow want? Strange how he wouldn't give his name.

"You're her boy, aren't you?" It sounded more like an accusation than a question.

"Yes. Bobby Ewing," he said, knowing enough by now not to extend his hand.

"You sure do take after Jock . . . you're built like him . . ."

Bobby didn't know how to take all this; he felt like a piece of livestock being sized up for auction.

"Damn! Damn! She went through with it after all!" the man exploded as if from nowhere, his voice rising like a tidal wave. "I kept hoping the rumors weren't true, that she'd back out of marrying him before it was too late. But you —you're the proof, aren't you. Dammit! That mean-spirited, hard-boiled oilman."

Suddenly Bobby had had enough. How dare this guy, no matter what his age, come into the house and start insulting his father to his face like that! "I think you'd better stop it right there, mister, before you have cause to regret what you're saying. This happens to be Jock Ewing's house, and you oughtn't to be calling him names right in front of it."

If the man hadn't been so old, Bobby might have become more physical, but his ingrown respect for elders held him back just enough to avoid a real fight. In any case, the old man was over his anger; just as quickly as it had come, it had gone.

"I'll be damned," he muttered, "it is Jock Ewing's house, isn't it." His strength seemed to have crumpled, and he turned to leave without another word.

His lady friend remained for a moment and said softly to Bobby, "We'll come again tonight."

Having heard her, the old man turned around

and barked at her to shut up. But she did not
back down, not a bit.

"We're coming back tonight," she said firmly
to her companion. "Deep down inside you want
to. You need to."

Without pausing to answer her, the old man
kept walking down the drive to where their car
was parked. The young lady lingered for a
moment. She wanted to apologize for the old
man's behavior.

"I'm sorry," Bobby began, "but I don't know
your name."

"Cathy. Cathy Baker." She smiled politely.

"Listen, Cathy, I don't get your friend there
. . . is he always so touchy?"

She shook her head sadly. "No . . . not
always . . . it's just that coming here is so difficult for him. It's important that he does it exactly
right, and that gets him on edge, you see . . .
it's—"

She was about to go on, but apparently
thought better of it. She turned and left quickly,
leaving behind her a deeply puzzled Bobby.

The pickup rolled down into the hollow, splash-
ing through the mud, and pulled up to the spot
where the ranchhands were busy laying drainage
pipe. The two men got out, and Ray led Jock
over to one of the hands, whom he introduced to
Jock as Ernie. Jock worked only with Ray, and
so introductions were needed. Once they had
shaken hands, Jock asked Ernie to tell him what
he had told Ray.

"Well, it was back a couple weeks or so," began Ernie. "I was over Section 40 way, rounding up some of the strays. It was a real hot, hazy day, you understand, right after sundown, and it was hard to make things out real clear at a distance. But I could swear I saw a truck out there by the well head."

"Well, was it a pickup, or what?" Jock barked.

"Oh, no, far's I could see, it looked like a tanker. In fact, hazy or not, I'd say it was a tanker for sure."

That was enough for Jock. He turned to Ray and waved him back to the truck. They were going to have a little look for themselves.

Section 40 was a deserted, Godforsaken part of Southfork Ranch, seemingly unremarkable except for the fact that it fronted on what used to be a back road. Now, across that back road, new condo units were being built as Dallas spread out to meet Fort Worth. Bobby had recently wanted to build a shopping center on Section 40 to serve those condos.

But what was really of interest to Jock was the oil—Section 40 stood over one of the largest oil deposits ever found in Texas. Jock had found it himself, years ago, when he was courting Miss Ellie, and Ellie's father, old man Southworth, had forbidden him or any other oilman from ever drilling on Southfork land. The old man had been a rancher through and through, and even though it had been during the Dust Bowl years, and the ranch had been close to bankruptcy, old man Southworth had held firm. In his old rancher's heart, oilmen were spoiling the land he loved, and he didn't intend to allow it on his ranch. In fact, he had been dead set against Ellie marrying Jock, but his daughter, who had always had her father wrapped around her little finger, had had her way. Nevertheless, Section 40 remained untapped. Or did it?

The two men hopped out onto the dusty ground, mostly dried clay with patches of scrub here and there, almost as brown as the dirt from the hot, dry summer.

Jock was deep in thought. "You know, Ray," he began, "a couple weeks back, me and J.R. and Bobby rode out here to look at where Bobby wanted to put that shopping center. Think Ernie could have mistaken a Mercedes for a tanker truck?"

It did not seem likely, but then, neither did any other explanation.

"Isn't this that well that's never supposed to be opened?"

"That's right, Ray," Jock said. "The old man made me promise before he died that nobody would ever drill for oil here, and now that I've become sort of a rancher myself, I feel the same way about it. Nobody's gonna drill for oil here while I'm alive. Or after. I've put it in my will."

But how could Jock know that his own son, J.R., had tampered with that will, so that after Jock's death he could drill to his heart's content, and that he was already making deals in exchange for that oil? In fact, it had been J.R.'s slow-witted partners, Jeb Ames and Willie Joe Garr, who had sent the team to check out the well's potential, the team whose tanker truck Ernie had spotted.

Ray and Jock poked around awhile, and finally, both men decided that nothing was out of the ordinary. Whatever the explanation, it was probably nothing unusual. A false alarm; nothing to worry about.

And then Ray saw it. A small, muddy pool of oil, half hidden in the scrub brush about sixteen feet from the well head.

Ray squatted down by the puddle, dipped his finger in, ran the greasy liquid between his thumb and finger and brought his fingers to his nose to smell it. Crude. He called Jock over to take a look.

Jock examined the liquid for himself, a puzzled expression on his face. He looked at Ray intently, then, without a word, strode back to the pickup and returned with a crowbar.

"Help me with this, Ray," he said as he walked over to the well head. "We're gonna raise this thing and see what's going on."

Ray got as good a grip as he could on the heavy wooden cover, and together, with a series of grunts, they succeeded in lifting it.

"Can you handle it if I let go and take a look?" Jock asked.

Ray nodded and Jock let go, moving to the side enough so that he could see the well head beneath them. With the sun shining down on it, the scratch marks made by some wrenches on the valve were obvious. Jock ran his hands over the tool and hammer marks, feeling the rough edges.

"This thing has been fooled with, all right," he muttered. "And whoever did it was mighty sloppy about it, too."

Ray looked at his boss quizzically. "Who would want to fool with it, Jock?"

The older man shook his head. "I haven't got a clue, Ray," he growled. "But I sure as hell am gonna get to the bottom of this."

Chapter Two

The Store was an immense place, the kind of place that overwhelmed its customers. Especially a pregnant shopper like Sue Ellen. After an hour or so of looking at cribs, bassinets, changing tables, swings, and other infant paraphernalia, both she and Miss Ellie were dizzy and more than ready to go to lunch and talk it over before deciding on any major purchases.

"I thought that crib would be just right in the nursery, Miss Ellie," Sue Ellen said as they breezed out onto the street. "You agree?"

"Completely," the older woman answered happily. Of course, even had she not thought so, she would have answered the same way. Being pregnant was so good for Sue Ellen, she was thinking. In the last few weeks she had been the happiest Ellie had seen her since the honeymoon.

Sue Ellen was thinking about wallpaper and

27

about whether or not it was right for the baby's room. She asked Miss Ellie if she liked a very cheerful pattern they'd seen back in the home furnishings department. Again, Miss Ellie was very enthusiastic, and Sue Ellen swelled with pleasure as she breathed deeply, smelling the roses planted just outside the door of The Store. For the first time in weeks, she felt no nausea, and she actually did feel like she had that glow that everyone associated with the expectant mother. She decided she would order the wallpaper right after lunch, before going back to Southfork.

Miss Ellie then asked what color Sue Ellen was going to order. This took Sue Ellen aback. She had not even considered the color.

She stopped in her tracks as the vision of Cliff Barnes swam before her eyes. Her lover, whom she could never be with again . . . And they were still in love, that was the tragedy of it all. But J.R. would never tolerate it—not with Cliff Barnes—and both she and Cliff had too much to lose . . . everything that meant anything to them . . . everything except each other.

She was suddenly seized by the desire to speak to Cliff, to communicate with him, to share this pregnancy with him. She was sure he was the father. It was so right, so just, so perfect. She hurriedly excused herself from Miss Ellie, saying she'd forgotten to make a phone call.

"Well, don't be long, Sue Ellen," Miss Ellie reminded her. "Pam ought to be here any minute. We're meeting her, remember?"

Sue Ellen had completely forgotten about Pam. That nervy Barnes girl! Pam had the temerity to marry into the Ewing family against almost everyone's wishes, and the way Miss Ellie accepted her! Made her feel like one of the family! Well, she thought, Pam had blown her chance to be the mother of the first grandson, and now it was going to be her turn, and Sue Ellen wasn't going to mess up.

She made for the phone booth and rang Cliff at his office. Sue Ellen listened to the phone ring on the other end of the line, and then spoke softly enough not to be overheard by Miss Ellie, who was windowshopping nearby.

Cliff Barnes was about to leave his office for lunch when the phone rang. He was wearing an old suit, one he had worn for years. But things were looking up now for Cliff. He had accepted a new appointment as head of the Office of Land Management, a powerful new environmental watchdog organization. He still didn't feel quite at home as the darling of the fat cats who had put him there, and who expected favors from him in return, but Cliff had decided to become a realist. No more would J.R. Ewing push him around with impunity. Cliff was going to fight back in earnest now and give the Ewings some of their own medicine, even if it meant he had to sell just a little of his soul to do it.

He picked up the phone, and Sue Ellen's voice hit him like a truck. It had been only two weeks since they had broken up, unable to overcome the reality of Sue Ellen's pregnancy, and she still burned in his heart like red-hot coals. His love for her came flooding back at the sound of her voice, and the tragedy of their parting seemed to drown his soul.

"I'm glad you answered the phone yourself instead of your secretary. Is she at lunch?"

"Yes," said Cliff. "Is something wrong? Why are you calling?"

"Oh, nothing's wrong, Cliff . . . but . . . what's your favorite color in the world?"

Cliff smiled. Was she going to get him a goodbye present? he wondered. "Oh, I don't know . . . I usually wear blues, grays and browns . . . you know, corporate colors . . . they're sure to please the big boys in the court-room or on the campaign trail. How's that?"

"I'm in a hurry, Cliff . . ." Sue Ellen whispered.

"Well," he answered, "then why don't you tell me what this is for?"

"It's for . . . it's for the baby's room," she said.

Cliff felt as though he'd been shot through the chest. His baby, his little new baby, would never know him . . . would never know that he was its father. He would never get to hold it, or to teach it how to stand, how to walk . . . no, it would be brought up by J.R. Ewing instead! The pain was almost unbearable.

Sue Ellen asked if he was still there.

"Light yellow," he said softly.

"I agree," said Sue Ellen. "I think it's the perfect choice."

"Please, Sue Ellen," pleaded Cliff. "Don't do this to me anymore, I beg you. I can't take it."

Sue Ellen felt her cheeks flush. "I . . . I'm sorry, darling," she whispered, a catch in her throat, "it's just that I find it so hard to think of never sharing with you again . . ."

Cliff nodded silently in understanding, but was unable to speak.

"I love you," she whispered, and then, "Goodbye." The line went dead.

Something inside Cliff seemed to go dead, too. It was over. Really over.

Sue Ellen stared at the dead receiver for a long moment, and then hung up. Seeing Miss Ellie windowshopping not far off, she made her way over to her.

"Miss Ellie," she said offhandedly, "I do believe that a light yellow would be just perfect for the nursery. Do you agree?"

Ellie smiled. "Sounds cheerful to me. What do you say we go on to the restaurant? I have a feeling Pam may be waiting for us."

Without another word, they walked quickly down the street.

Jock came down the stairs dressed in his dinner jacket, the one he usually wore to supper at Southfork, and made his way into the living room, where the family always gathered before taking their seats in the dining room.

J.R. and Bobby were already there, cocktails in hand. It pleased Jock to see his boys socializing together. His dream had always been that

J.R. and Bobby would run Ewing Oil together, but that just didn't seem to be working out. J.R. wasn't about to share his secrets with anybody. He kept the management of Ewing Oil very much to himself, so that half the time Jock wondered whether something fishy was going on. In the end, though, he consoled himself with the knowledge that whatever J.R. was doing over there at the office, it was resulting in the continued health and growth of the company Jock had founded.

Now, however, Jock was troubled. That well over on Section 40—something was weird about it. He decided to speak to J.R. about it immediately. While Bobby made him a light drink, Jock told J.R. about his and Ray's finding the pool of oil near the old well head. He watched his son for the telltale signs of guilt, but if J.R. had had anything to do with it, he wasn't showing it. He reacted with cool surprise to the news, not overreacting, nor trying to explain the condition of the capped well. He didn't doubt what Jock was saying but didn't put too much weight on it either.

"I had a good look at the well head itself," Jock went on, "and there's no mistake about it—I saw fresh scratches and hammer marks on that valve."

Bobby, returning with Jock's bourbon and branch, mostly branch, wondered aloud about why anyone would want to tamper with the old well. Any kind of profitable tapping would surely be noticed before it could get very far.

Jock shook his head, saying he couldn't figure it out for the life of him. Then he turned to J.R. and pointedly asked him if he had any ideas about what could have happened. Jock couldn't have said why, but he had the unshakable feeling that J.R. knew more about the well than he was letting on.

J.R. took a long moment to consider Jock's question and then said, "Well, you know, now that I think of it, isn't that well kind of close to the road back there? The public road? Seems to me it could very well have been just a little plain ordinary everyday vandalism. I'll tell you what, I'll have it looked into, Daddy."

Jock patted his son on the shoulder. The message was clear. If J.R. had had nothing to do with it, he'd find out what had happened. If he had, nothing more would happen now that Jock had served notice that he was watching out for the well.

"Let me know what you find out, boy," Jock said, smiling.

J.R. smiled too, but his heart was black with anger. Those stupid roughnecks! They'd nearly caused him a heap of trouble.

"May we come in, boys, or are women not allowed at this little party?" It was Miss Ellie, still aglow from her happy day with her daughters-in-law. Behind her were Pam and Sue Ellen, and Lucy brought up the rear.

"Well, lookie here, Daddy, Bobby—I see some pretty ladies over there—what say we invite 'em in?"

J.R. moved to the bar to pour drinks for the ladies, while all the others settled around the sofa and chairs to wait for dinner.

It was then that Bobby remembered the unexplained visitors. "Momma," he began, "there was somebody here to see you this afternoon —an older man, very strange guy . . ."

Ellie's eyebrows lifted in surprise. "What was his name, Bobby?"

"That's part of what was so strange," Bobby answered, shaking his head. "He wouldn't say . . ."

Now Jock was beginning to become intrigued. "You keepin' secrets from your husband, Ellie?" he joked.

Ellie, of course, knew he was teasing. There could never be any question of Ellie being less than completely loyal. It was not in her nature. Nevertheless, she blushed. "Oh, be quiet, Jock! Really!"

Bobby went over to the corner of the room where he had put the package the visitor had left, and brought it over to his mother. "He brought this for you. It's a present, I believe."

This was all too much for Lucy, whose naughty little mind was imagining all sorts of intrigue. "Grandma's got a boyfriend, I just know it!" She giggled happily.

"I wouldn't be too sure of that, Lucy," Bobby said. "You should have gotten a load of the young lady he had with him."

Ellie, meanwhile, had been removing the brown paper from around the painting, and now stood silently looking at it, gaping in shock.

The family gathered around behind her to get a better look, but only Jock seemed to recognize the house in the painting. The others were merely curious.

"Grandma, what does it mean?" asked Lucy, not a little troubled by her grandmother's reaction. "Do you recognize the house?"

Jock broke in, answering for his nonplussed wife. "That's Southfork, Lucy," he said softly.

Now Ellie found her voice. "It's the old house . . . the one we lived in before Jock and I met . . ." She shook herself out of her stupor. "Bobby, are you positive this man didn't say his name, or where he could be reached, or anything at all?"

Bobby nodded. The man had made a point of keeping his identity a secret.

"What I can't figure out," said Jock, scratching his cheek, "is who could possibly remember what that house looked like, except for Ellie, and me, and Digger Barnes . . ."

Ellie looked at him warily. Digger Barnes had been Ellie's beau before she had met Jock, and Jock and Digger had been enemies even before Jock had stolen Ellie's heart.

But Bobby knew Digger—he was his father-in-law, after all—so it couldn't have been him.

The doorbell rang, and everyone looked over that way.

"I guess we'll find out now," said Bobby. "He did say he'd be coming again this evening to say hello."

Raoul crossed the entryway and opened the door.

The huge shadow of a man covered the open doorway, and a gravelly voice outside said, "I'm here to see Ellie Southworth—I mean Ewing."

The voice shook Ellie. Trembling, she rose out of her chair, framed by her family, which had gathered behind her. She could not believe the voice was real . . . it was impossible . . . it could not be . . .

Raoul entered the living room, and behind him could be seen the hulking figure of Garrison. He moved past Raoul, then stood still, looking solemnly at Ellie, who had not moved an inch since she'd heard his voice.

"Garrison!" she gasped in wonder.

He nodded humbly. "Yes, it's me, Ellie."

The whole family stood there, confused, except for Jock, who obviously recognized the stranger, and just as obviously was less than pleased to see him again.

Ellie stood rooted to the spot where she stood. "But . . . but . . . you're dead! You've been dead for forty years! How . . . I thought . . ."

Garrison nodded sadly. "Yes, I wanted you to believe I was dead. I'm sorry that it caused you pain, but it was the only way I knew . . . I had to do it."

Bobby was becoming more and more perplexed, and, as there was now a moment of silence, he looked inquiringly at his mother.

"Bobby, J.R., everybody," she said slowly, "this is Garrison Southworth . . . my brother."

The silence that followed was the unmistakable calm before the storm. For about five seconds you could have heard a pin drop before everyone began expressing their surprise and shock out loud. Pam and Sue Ellen had not even known Miss Ellie had a brother. The others had heard only vague stories about him and had always seen him as sort of a historic figure. And now, here he was in the flesh, as large as life, or even larger.

Ellie was unable to take the few small steps that separated her from her brother. She stood there, trembling, tears coursing down her cheeks, with a dumbfounded expression on her face. It was as if she had seen a ghost; indeed, she literally had. For her, the room and all its occupants had faded away, and she and Garrison stood facing each other as if the years had never come between them, as if in a dream. But this was no dream; this was real.

For his part, Garrison seemed extremely uncomfortable. He had prepared long and hard for this moment, and yet returning to Southfork and seeing Ellie were even more difficult than he had ever imagined they would be.

Miss Ellie found her voice again. "They told us you went down with your ship in that storm . . . we held a big memorial service for you, and all I could think of the whole time was how horrible it must be to drown, with the water closing in all around you, and your lungs screaming for air . . ."

Garrison's expression grew even more pained. "I'm sorry," he said again, "I knew this was going to be hard for me . . . I didn't realize how hard it would be for you, Ellie . . ."

But for Miss Ellie, as for her brother, it was not only pain, but joy, that she felt. "I still can't believe it," she whispered, "and Garrison, do you know that after forty years, I still would have known you on the street!"

Jock had come up behind her, seriously concerned for his wife's well-being. She was shaking so violently and seemed so fragile somehow. "Why don't you sit down for a minute," he suggested, whispering it tenderly in her ear.

But it was as if Ellie did not hear him at all. "First Daddy died," she intoned, "and then, so soon after . . . you. It was almost too much to bear . . ."

Garrison felt himself jumping out of his skin with guilt and sorrow. "Please try to understand, Ellie . . . all that misery . . . the dust storms and the dead cattle everywhere, and the ranch about to go broke . . . and all those fights Daddy and I kept having over every little thing. I know I abandoned you to handle everything alone. I just couldn't handle the responsibility, and later, once I'd gone away, I couldn't face you. I thought I could never face you again . . . but . . . well . . . here I am."

Suddenly she remembered how it had been to lose him. And to think that all that time he'd been alive, that he could have come back to her!

"Oh!" she gasped. "How? How could you do such a thing?"

Again, all Garrison could say was, "I'm so sorry . . . forgive me, Ellie, please."

As suddenly as her anger had come, it disap-

peared, and all that was left was the huge wave
of relief and gratitude that her brother had come
back to her. "It's a dream . . . a dream!" she
cried, stepping toward and throwing her arms
around him like a starving man embracing a
meal.

They hugged and hugged, while around them
the rest of the family, the tension finally broken,
asked each other what had happened, what the
others knew about all this. Jock explained that
Garrison had been in the Merchant Marine, but
could go no further. He, too, was flabbergasted
that the dead man had come miraculously back
to life.

Pam suddenly realized that she had heard
stories about Garrison Southworth from her
father. But her father hadn't talked about Miss
Ellie's brother for many years now.

J.R. was trying to get Ellie to respond to his
questions about Uncle Garrison. Was he the one
she used to tell him stories about when it was his
bedtime? He remembered stories of the sea
—fantastic, Sinbad-like stories. So this was
Uncle Garrison in the flesh. Well, well, well . . .

Sue Ellen, ever the perfect hostess, remarked
that perhaps Uncle Garrison would like to sit
down, and that perhaps J.R. ought to get him a
drink. Reminded of his social obligations, J.R.
asked his uncle what he could get him, and
Garrison said he'd have a glass of wine.

Then it occurred to the old man that he hadn't
met any of the others, who, after all, were his
family too. "What's your name, son?" he asked.

"I'm J.R., sir, John Junior, Jock and Ellie's oldest boy . . . will that be red wine or white, sir?"

Garrison shrugged, not caring one way or the other. He separated himself from Ellie's grasp and walked over to Jock.

"Jock Ewing," he mused. "Let me tell you something. I was in New York City, about to board ship for the first time in my life, when I picked up a newspaper and read about you and Ellie getting hitched . . . I damn near lost my lunch! I can just imagine how Digger Barnes took the news . . . he must have keeled over stone dead!"

Jock shook his head. "Still alive, I'm afraid," he said with a wry smile.

"Well, now, will wonders never cease!" said Garrison, happy to hear it.

"He's alive, all right," chirped Pam, attracting Garrison's notice for the first time.

"Well, now," he said, going over to her, "and who is this lovely young lady?"

"My name's Pamela, Pamela Ewing—I'm Digger Barnes' daughter. Bobby Ewing's my husband."

Garrison took a moment to think about this. He smiled to think of a Barnes married to a Ewing. What a supreme irony. If he'd have known about it, he might have come back to Dallas sooner, just to see Jock's discomfiture.

"You must have been overjoyed about that one, huh, Jock," he said, not even trying to hide his dislike for his brother-in-law.

Jock, for the moment, did not allow himself to be bothered by the taunt.

J.R., however, who now gave Garrison his drink, was curious. "I gather that you and Digger Barnes were close, then?" he prompted.

"Bosom buddies, I'd call it," answered Garrison. "I kept trying to talk him into coming with me, dropping all this oil stuff and going out to sea. I still think he would have been happier . . . although," he remarked, looking at Pam, "I guess if he'd have come, you wouldn't be here, would you?"

Jock had had enough of Garrison's abrasiveness. "He's been gone for forty years, and he's got nothing to say except to talk about Barnes!" he fumed.

Garrison smiled. "Still feuding, eh, Jock? I'd have thought you'd have buried the hatchet by now, considering you're related by marriage!"

Pam smiled. She liked this old man, who didn't seem in the least intimidated by Jock Ewing. "Feuding is meat and potatoes to some people," she remarked offhandedly.

Garrison smiled at the brave young lady who, Barnes that she was, had had the guts to marry a Ewing and live at Southfork. "Is Digger a granddaddy yet, or have you been sleeping on the job?" he teased.

"We're waiting on it awhile," said Pam, blushing just a bit.

"Well, don't wait too long, young lady . . . I know Digger would just love to have a grandchild!"

Sue Ellen choked on her drink, coughing violently. Digger Barnes was in all probability the grandfather of *her* child! "So clumsy of me!" she apologized, trying to catch her breath.

"Sue Ellen's pregnant," Lucy explained. "They say it makes you act funny sometimes. Sure does with Sue Ellen!"

"Nonsense, Lucy!" Sue Ellen corrected her sharply. "I'm just fine. Swallowed the wrong way is all." She turned away, ostensibly to compose herself, but really to hide the fact that she was blushing a deep red.

J.R. now saw his opening. "Well, Uncle Garrison, what prompted you to come back to Southfork now?"

Taking the question for what it was worth, Garrison tried to give an honest answer without really telling them the whole truth. "Well, it wasn't an easy thing to do, even after all these years," he confessed. "I did a lot of thinking about it, and Cathy and I talked about it a lot."

"Cathy . . . is that your wife, Garrison?" Ellie interrupted him.

"No, she's not my wife. I'm not married . . . never did get married, as a matter of fact. Cathy Baker is my . . ." He stopped short, searching for the right words. "She's my very close friend," he said finally. It wasn't a lie, anyhow, even if it wasn't the true story. "For a long time now, I've had a very strong desire to see my childhood home, and an even stronger urge to see my sister."

Ellie still gaped at her brother's form, not quite able to realize that he was really there in front of her, that it wasn't all just a dream. However, from outward appearances, she seemed to have calmed down considerably.

J.R. was not finished with his inquisition. "I suppose it was your good friend Cathy who suggested this little visit in the first place."

Garrison looked hard at J.R., not really sure what he was trying to insinuate. "She was for it, if that's what you mean. She could see that I really wanted to do it, deep down inside. But it was my idea to begin with."

J.R. seemed deep in thought for a moment, ambling toward Garrison in a roundabout arc. "Seems to me, from the stories I've been told—" he shot a glance at his mother "—that ranching didn't appeal to you much, that you couldn't wait to get away from Southfork."

"Well," mused Garrison, "that was true then . . . now things are a little bit different. Age changes a lot about a man . . . I guess I'm no different. It changes the way you look at a lot of things."

J.R. paced back and forth across the floor, as if he were a lawyer in the middle of a cross-examination. He was obviously getting around to something. "So you feel now that you want the ranch again?" he asked.

"That I want to *see* it again," Garrison corrected him.

"And to see Ellie."

Garrison turned to his sister, not wanting to be

drawn into whatever snake pit J.R. was preparing for him. "It's really astounding, how much everything's changed . . . this new house. It's very impressive, imposing even . . . so much grander than the old clapboard ranch house we used to live in."

"Much grander even than you thought it might be, isn't that right, sir?" It was J.R. again. He was dangerously close to causing a scene, but he seemed not to care. He was his usual unflappable self, and he seemed to want to ruffle his uncle's feathers, to see what lay beneath this visit.

Ellie saw the brewing anger in her brother's stiff posture, and she rushed in to change the subject before he blew up and the visit was ruined.

"Oh, Garrison. Tell me the whole story. I want to know all about what you've been doing all those years! Your life must have been very exciting."

But Garrison had gathered himself to leave. "I'll come back again in the morning, Ellie. Tomorrow, I'll tell you the whole dull story." He went to embrace her, and, looking over her shoulder at Jock and J.R., he added, "I've obviously stayed longer than I should have already."

Ellie took him by the arms and pushed him back so she could see his face again. "Why don't you stay the night with us?" she pleaded, sensing that he wouldn't in any case.

"I can't, Ellie," he replied. "Cathy is expecting

me back at the hotel." And with that he started for the door, closely followed by his sister, who clung to him, as if she were afraid he might be taken from her yet again.

The family watched them go and then turned their attention to each other.

Lucy approached her uncle Bobby, her curiosity ablaze. Her father, the middle Ewing brother, had also run away, unable to take the pressures of living at Southfork with the Ewings. She missed him terribly, and Garrison was a reminder of him.

"Did they name my daddy after Uncle Garrison, Bobby?"

Bobby took a moment to think about it. "I don't know, Lucy," he answered, "but it would sure seem like it, wouldn't it?"

"In that case," said Lucy, "I like Uncle Garrison a whole lot."

In the far corner of the room, over by the bar, J.R. was freshening his drink, and his father's. Both men had wry smiles on their faces, but the concern was etched deeply underneath.

"Daddy, I don't know about you," J.R. said softly as he dropped the ice cubes into his father's drink, "but I think this might turn out to be a troublesome little visit. Uncle Garrison might need a little careful handling."

Jock stared at the front door, where Ellie was kissing her brother good-bye. "Don't worry about Garrison, son," he said. "Whatever he's after, we'll handle him."

Chapter Three

It was the next morning, and the sun shone brightly through the white curtains of Bobby and Pam's bedroom. Bobby emerged from the shower, a towel draped around his shoulders, his body mostly dry now, except for a few droplets that glistened as the sun hit them.

Pam watched her husband from the bed, pleased by how handsome he was, by the way his muscles rippled under his taut, suntanned skin. They had made love late last night, and now Pam felt tired from lack of sleep.

"You can have the bathroom now," he said over his shoulder.

"I'm not getting out of this bed. Not till this afternoon at least." Reaching toward him, she whispered, "Come here."

Bobby sat down on the edge of the bed and gazed down into his wife's misty eyes, the message in them unmistakable. He kissed her languorously, caressing her face as he did so.

"Are you trying to get me to play hooky?" he asked.

"Something like that," she answered, a kitten-ish smile curving her lips.

Bobby considered it for a moment, but it was impossible. "I really would like to . . . I mean I *really* would . . . but I can't. Not today. I've got four meetings, and I can't put off any of them."

"Darn," she swore softly. She had to face the fact that just because she had the morning off, it didn't mean Bobby did too. Oh, well, that was the price of being married to the man she loved. If they'd still been dating, he would have stayed.

"I'll take a rain check," she said, giving him one last loving caress.

Sighing, he managed to extricate himself from the bed.

"Wasn't that amazing last night." She smiled, recalling the previous night's turn of events. "I've never seen Miss Ellie so wired! She just went on and on till . . . what was it, two o'clock?"

Bobby grinned, remembering. His mother's excitement had been infectious, at least on the two of them and Lucy. "Can you imagine not seeing your brother for forty years, thinking he was dead, and then, *bang!*" he mused. "No wonder she was excited!"

"I have a vague memory," Pam said, "of my father talking about this sailor friend of his . . . he used to tell me how this man was going to go all around the world, from one end to the other. The way he talked about him, I remember thinking how much he would have liked to have gone. I think he might have done it, too, if he hadn't been such an oil junkie . . ."

"Well," said Bobby, "it's a darn good thing he didn't go off to sea, because then where would *you* be?"

She smiled and pulled him down to her again. "Keep it up, buster, and I'm never gonna let you out of my arms." And she kissed him till the world seemed to disappear.

Across the hall, in another bedroom, Sue Ellen sat at her vanity chair applying her makeup, while J.R. stood by the full-length mirror knotting his tie. Both of them seemed preoccupied, each in his or her own world.

Finally, Sue Ellen was satisfied with the results of her work and turned to face her husband. "Well, wasn't that something last night . . . long-lost relatives surfacing, coming back from the dead."

J.R. had been thinking about much the same thing. "I think he came back to get the ranch away from us, that's what I think."

Sue Ellen straightened up in shock. She had had an inkling this was the case, but until now she hadn't taken it seriously. It was a nightmarish thought. "But . . . he can't do that, can he? How could he do something like that?"

J.R. slipped on his suit jacket as he spoke. "Daddy was telling me that in Grandpa South-worth's will, the ranch was left to Garrison, one hundred per cent. Of course, when the news came that he was drowned, Momma got the ranch by default."

Sue Ellen's jaw was set in defiance. That old sailor was not going to get Southfork away from her. The ranch was going to be her child's inheritance, and nobody was going to take it away from them!

"Is it possible he could get Southfork away from us, J.R.?" she asked angrily.

"Don't worry your little head about it, Sue Ellen," J.R. said, looking at her in the mirror. "Nobody's going to come in here and take South-fork. This is Ewing property, and that's how it's gonna stay. You just leave it to me and don't think twice about it. Soon as I get another little matter taken care of, I'm gonna see about Uncle Garrison. See you tonight, darlin'." Finished, he left the room.

Sue Ellen looked after him, only a little com-forted. If there were only something *she* could do . . .

Ray was down in a gully, supervising the hands as they piled drainage pipes into the racks that would hold them. It was dirty, hot, sweaty work, and all the men, including Ray, had their shirts off. It was practically a mud pit, an ugly scene, and so, when Ray spotted J.R.'s spotless new Mercedes in the distance, rolling down the dirt road toward them, he spit on the ground in anger.

Typical J.R. Always thinking he was better than everybody else, always messin' in other people's lives. Ray hated him. And to think they'd once been buddies. That had been before J.R. had stolen Ray's girlfriend, singer Garnet McGee. J.R. stopped at nothing to get what he wanted. Not even hurting his friends or his family.

J.R. stepped out of the car and made his way over toward where Ray was standing. He strode carefully, avoiding the mud puddles that lay everywhere, trying to keep his boots shiny.

Ray wiped his hands on his brow, getting the stinging sweat out of his eyes. He did not offer his hand to J.R. J.R., he knew, would not take it anyway.

"Ray, I want to talk to you," said J.R., ominously.

So J.R. was mad at him, for who knew what reason. Well, Ray was mad at him, too! He was not going to let J.R. intimidate him. Not anymore.

Before walking off with J.R., he turned to his hands. "Be back in a minute, okay?" To them he would show courtesy. They were working people, the salt of the earth—honest, simple men, who would never, ever think of stabbing other people in the back, of treading over them in order to get what they wanted.

He followed J.R. a few steps away, until they were out of earshot.

"Well, what do you want, J.R.?" he asked peremptorily.

J.R. removed his hat to straighten his hair, and regarded Ray sternly. "You realize, Ray, that you got my daddy all worked up over nothing about those grease stains you found over Section 40?" His gaze would have shattered glass, but he was trying to seem casual, as if it were a minor matter.

Ray knew better. J.R. wouldn't have come all the way out to this ditch just to talk to him about minor matters.

"It wasn't grease, J.R.," Ray said, standing firm. "It was oil."

"I see," J.R. replied skeptically, "and you say it was *you* who found the oil. You personally."

"That's right." Ray put his hands on his hips, waiting for J.R.'s next move.

"Well, then, if you say it was oil, it must have been oil. I'll bet one of our pickups has got a leak in it. You go tell the mechanic to check each and every one of 'em."

Ray stood staring at J.R. Something was fishy. J.R. was deliberately trying to minimize this, trying to make him think he hadn't seen what he knew he'd seen.

"This was a puddle of crude oil, J.R., not motor oil."

J.R. laughed loudly, mirthlessly. His voice dripping with sarcasm, he remarked, "Listen to you, Ray. You're a cowboy—a good one, I admit, but still, a cowboy—you don't know an oil well from a hole in the ground. Don't tell me what's crude and what isn't. You just tell the mechanic to take those trucks apart and find that leak. It'll be there, I bet you anything."

J.R. started to walk off toward his car, then turned, adding, "Oh, and Ray—from now on, if you come up against anything relating to oil, you just come to me with it, all right? Leave my daddy alone. He's retired now, and I don't want him bothered with things like that. Momma wouldn't like it either." And with that, he was gone.

Ray frowned deeply. Something was very suspicious. Had J.R. not come to him and tried to steer him away from the track, he probably would have forgotten all about it. But now he was sure that J.R. was up to something, and whatever it was, it was something J.R. didn't want anybody to know about. That meant trouble, and Ray decided that he was going to get to the bottom of it. J.R. was right about one thing; Ray couldn't bother Jock and Ellie about it. Not until he had absolute proof.

Turning back to the ranchhands, Ray excused himself, saying he'd be back later. He then hopped into the pickup and drove off, in search of answers.

Louella, J.R.'s secretary, and sometimes more than that, was just putting the finishing touches on the office. J.R. wasn't often late for work, and this was a rare opportunity for her to organize the place. She had just replenished his supply of pads and pencils when he walked in, obviously agitated and in a great hurry.

"Good morning, J.R.," she said.

"Mmm," he replied, not really listening. "Louella, darlin', would you get me Willie Joe Garr on the phone right away? Thank you, babe." And without waiting for her to reply, he went over to the bar to fix himself a drink.

Louella left the room, and, drink in hand, J.R. walked over to the window and looked out into the distance, the Dallas skyline and the wide Texas horizon beyond staring him in the face. It was, in more ways than one, his kingdom, and he didn't intend to let it get away from him. Not on account of two fools like Ames and Garr.

The intercom buzzer sounded, and J.R. went to pick up the phone. "Willie Joe? . . . get Jeb on the other line. I want to talk to both of you . . ." He heard the other man's voice as he got on the line. "You fellas have succeeded in causing me a lot of trouble. That so-called inspection team of yours left a pool of oil behind it. One of the hands found it and showed it off to my daddy. Now that was sloppy work, boys. Real sloppy."

He stopped for a moment. Ames and Garr were worried about the repercussions for their secret deal to pump oil at Southfork after Jock's death.

"Now, don't worry about it," J.R. assured them. "I've got the situation under control—for now. But don't screw me up again with your stupidity, y'hear? If you can't be a help, at least stay out of the way, understand?"

They did.

J.R. hung up, feeling a little more peaceful

now that he'd spoken his mind. He proceeded to turn his attention to his Uncle Garrison.

Out on the back porch, Ellie and Jock were whiling the time away playing backgammon, drinking coffee while they waited for Garrison to show up. Jock, for a change, was winning. They had played for years, and he could still count the number of times he'd won. Miss Ellie was a superior player, and yet this morning he seemed to be winning with ease. Miss Ellie's attention was obviously wandering from the game, and Jock thought he knew where.

"Ellie," he complained, putting down the dice, "it's no fun for me to win if it's no big deal for you to lose."

The joke was lost on Ellie, but she could tell that Jock was annoyed that her mind was elsewhere. To avoid an argument, she proceeded to include him in her thoughts. She had been remembering the hearing, long ago, when she had petitioned to have Garrison declared legally dead. It was at Jock's instigation that she had initiated proceedings, and she had felt awful about it. Now that Garrison was alive again, she was feeling even worse.

Jock pointed out to her that, at the time, the ranch had been tied up in legal knots, due to old man Southworth's death, and that the only way Southfork could have been saved was to have it go to Ellie, the only remaining member of the family who could be responsible for it.

There was no arguing with Jock's logical

points, but that didn't make Ellie feel any better. Somehow, with Garrison alive after all, it seemed to her as if she had stolen the ranch from her brother all those years ago.

Jock soon saw that it was impossible to reason with Ellie about it, that it was purely an emotional matter with her, and so he determined to leave her alone with her ruminations, lest his arguing make it even worse. He rose to go, saying that he had decided to have lunch at the club.

"Oh, no, Jock," she protested, "please stay! Garrison's going to be here soon!"

Jock wavered for a moment, wondering how to be tactful about this. Garrison obviously couldn't stand him, and he still claimed his friendship with Digger Barnes. There was no sense in sitting around pretending he and Garrison liked each other.

"He's coming to see you, Ellie, not me," he finally said. "You'll be able to talk a lot more freely without me around."

As tactful as he had tried to be, his words still upset Miss Ellie.

"Oh, Jock. I wish I knew what you have against him."

"That's not how it is, not at all, Ellie. It's the other way round . . . remember, when I came into the picture, I was a total outsider. He and Digger, they were already buddies. They both resented my success . . . and neither one of them could deal with it. And so they both retreated . . . one went to sea, and the other went to seed."

Miss Ellie shook her head. "Jock, you're not being fair!" she protested.

Jock sighed sadly. "Maybe you're right, Ellie," he said, shaking his head. "I sincerely hope you are. But Garrison looks to me like a man out to get his hands on something. Something that isn't his . . . I've seen that look a thousand times, and I believe I'd know it anywhere. I'm sorry if that shocks you, but I've got to call 'em like I see 'em. If I'm wrong, and all he wants is to see you, then I'll be the first to admit it. I'll be more than happy to apologize if what I'm thinking is wrong —but like I said, I don't think it is."

Dallas is an oil town first, and a cattle town second. Or, it's a cattle town first, and an oil town second. That means the cowboys have almost nothing to do with the roughnecks, as the oil workers are known. They keep to different bars, live in different neighborhoods, and have very little in common with each other. So for Ray Krebbs to be haunting roughneck watering holes was unusual to say the least, and he attracted a lot of attention.

It took him a long time to find what he was looking for, and when he did, it happened pretty much by accident. He had wandered into a beer bar at about four in the afternoon, much too early to see any real action, or try to pin anybody down. The only patrons were a few roughnecks with their women, sitting at isolated plastic tables in various corners of the establishment. Ray had stopped in only on an impulse. He'd been passing by, felt thirsty, and decided to try to get two birds with one stone. But as so often happens, it was at the unlikeliest time that he got lucky, and his old buddy Matt walked into the bar. Matt was in his mid-thirties, a burly sort, but obviously not mean or aggressive. He and Ray had worked together on a project for Ewing Oil at a time when both Jock and J.R. were busy with bigger deals, and Bobby was still at school. Ray had been a sort of foreman-in-training, and Matt had taken him under his wing, showing him the ropes.

Ray greeted him warmly and got a bear hug in return. "Let me buy you a beer, big fella," Ray said, drawing him over to a table.

Matt wondered aloud whether Ray was trying to get his butt kicked, showing up at a rough-neck bar. When they had chewed the fat for a few minutes and were halfway into their beers, Ray asked Matt if he'd heard about any oil drilling on Southfork Ranch. "I know you know everybody there is to know in the fields, and I thought maybe you could help me," he said.

"Well, I sure would if I could, good buddy," Matt apologized, "but I haven't heard a whisper about anything like that. Not a word, and believe me, I'd have heard about something like that!"

But Ray was not taking no for an answer. Before leaving his old friend, he elicited a promise from him to ask around and see if he could find out anything. When Matt asked him why he wanted to know so badly, Ray merely shook his head. When hunting J.R. Ewing, a man had to be very quiet.

Garrison arrived shortly after Jock's departure, and seemed not to miss his presence in the least. It was indeed Ellie he had come to see, and it turned out just as well that Jock had decamped. Ellie showed him into the house and gave him the grand tour. Southfork was now an impressive mansion, and Garrison kept shaking his head, thinking of the ramshackle old house they had once called home.

When the tour was over, she brought him into the living room, and as they sat down to recover, she asked him again about staying at Southfork.

"Oh, well, Ellie, I don't think Cathy would agree to stay here," he said.

Ellie didn't understand why not, and he couldn't—or wouldn't—explain it to her. Nor would he say whether he was serious about the woman named Cathy.

"I don't want to talk about me now, Ellie," he protested. "Let's you and me talk about old times. I remember how wonderful it was to grow up here at Southfork. Time hasn't taken that away . . . but I must say, big and grand as this house is, it still has that wonderful feeling about it. And the ranch looks better than it ever has, from what I saw driving out here on the Braddock road."

Ellie sat listening to him, gazing raptly at his grizzled sailor's face with the salt-and-pepper beard. She could see, beneath the lines and the beard, the young man's face she had once known and loved. It was still Garrison, still her brother.

"Things were so bad when you went away . . ." she mused. "The thirties were a terrible time . . . so many of the ranches went under."

Garrison knew she was trying to understand why he had left in the middle of the depression, why he had run away, leaving her to fend for herself.

"Ellie, I loved our father. You know that . . . I loved him much more than I could say at the time. But I didn't understand that he loved me back. That look in his eyes every time he had to go auction off some of the stock . . . they weren't bringing in hardly any money at all at the time, remember? That awful empty look he had . . . and there I was, his only son, twenty years old, strong as an ox, and totally helpless! There was nothing I could do for him . . . and he'd shout at me all the time, out of his frustration. I remember that, in spite of everything, he kept acting like the lord of the manor, as if things had never been better around here. I remember his voice, so tough and gravelly, but then there was that hidden edge of fear underneath it all. I don't think he even heard it himself, but I know I did. It was in his eyes, too . . . stark, naked fear."

He paused to wipe the beginnings of tears from his eyes. "I couldn't stand to see one more dying steer covered with dust, the dust that was always in your eyes and mouth. I had to get out of here . . . I had to believe that things were better somewhere out there . . . and I had to find that better world for myself. Can you understand that?"

Ellie was looking at her shoes now, but her eyes had a faraway look as she relived the most awful time of her life.

"Why did you let out the word that you were dead? Didn't you know how hard it would hit me, with Daddy only four months gone?"

"I only did what I thought was best," he replied softly. "I knew that you had married Jock Ewing, and I also knew that with his money, the ranch would recover, and prosper, and grow. I didn't want to jeopardize that—it was Daddy's heart and soul—and besides, I would only have run it into the ground myself. Even Daddy always said that I made a lousy rancher. Try to imagine it, Ellie. There I was in Europe, having the time of my life, happy for the first time in years, with lots of adventure and excitement. Coming back would have meant I was nothing but a servant to Jock Ewing. I couldn't have stood that. It just wasn't in me."

Ellie interrupted him, pointing out that if their daddy had thought him such a terrible rancher, he wouldn't have left Southfork solely to him.

"Look, Ellie, it turned out for the best," he said soothingly. "You've got the ranch and your family and all you could ever want. And I . . . I've lived the life I always wanted to live. Tell me," he said, changing the subject, "have I already met the whole family, or are there more of them squirreled away somewhere?"

"I have one more son—Lucy's father—his name is Gary." She paused to smile. "We named him after you. And it's funny, Garrison, but the two of you are very much like each other. Gary's very much a drifter, a wanderer . . ."

"Well," said Garrison, patting her knee reassuringly, "at least one of the wanderers has come home to roost, for now."

Miss Ellie's brow creased with worry. "For now? You don't mean you're not staying? Oh, Garrison, you must! This is your home!"

"No, Ellie," he said, shaking his head, "I've missed you and Southfork more than I can say. But it's changed. It isn't the home I left behind all those years ago. In a sense, I don't really have a home anywhere anymore."

"Oh, yes you do, Garrison," Ellie insisted. "You do have a home—and this is it."

Late that night, after dinner, Ellie called her husband and sons into the den, saying she had something important to tell them.

The men got drinks for themselves and sat down, but they were all on edge. Each of them suspected, to a greater or lesser degree, that Miss Ellie was going to tell them that she had invited Garrison to stay at Southfork for good.

"Well, let's get on with it, Momma," prompted J.R., "before we all bite our nails off."

Ellie stood before them, gathering her strength. "This is not going to be easy for me," she began, understating the case. "I love you all very much, and I also love Southfork. I suppose you all know that Garrison was named sole heir to the ranch when my daddy died, and that Jock and I had to declare him legally dead in order for the title to pass to me.

"Well, now Garrison's back, alive, and I have to do what my conscience tells me is fair and right. It pains me, but I feel I have no choice. I've decided to give Southfork back to Garrison."

Chapter Four

The men were thunderstruck. In their wildest dreams, they had never imagined this possibility. That Garrison might try to get the ranch back, yes, even that he might try to manipulate Miss Ellie, but that she would come, of her own free will, to the decision she had reached was unthinkable. Yet she had done just that.

"What the hell kind of upside-down thinking is that!" Jock bellowed. "You can't give Garrison Southfork!"

Ellie stood firm, her jaw set with determination. "I've always felt, deep inside, that I stole the ranch from him. That hearing . . . never finding the body . . . even all the while we thought he was dead, I never felt quite right about it."

"What about me, Miss Ellie?" Jock insisted. "I poured everything I had into saving this ranch —my money, my sweat, my heart. What did

Garrison ever do for Southfork? The place was bankrupt when I got here, and if it had been up to Garrison, it would have stayed that way!"

"I know how you feel, Jock," Ellie soothed him. "I understand all of that, and it's all true—every word of it. But in spite of everything, the ranch really belongs to Garrison. If we hadn't wrongly declared him dead, the ranch would still be his. We've got to give it back to him."

Now it was the boys' turn to speak up. Bobby remarked that while Garrison had grown up there, so had they, and that it was their home she was talking about giving away, not just theoretically, but for real. J.R. reiterated Jock's point that Garrison could never have saved the ranch had he stayed to defend it from the auction block. As far as J.R. was concerned, even if it had been wrong to begin with, so much time had passed that the field now belonged, by right, to the ones who used it, to the ones who had occupied it for forty years.

But Ellie was adamant, sticking to her position with unaccustomed stubbornness. Obviously this was a moral imperative for her, and she felt there was no getting around it.

"Wrongs can be righted," she insisted, "no matter how much time has passed. When my daddy died and left the ranch to my brother, and to him alone, I was upset. I never let on to you, Jock, but I felt hurt that my daddy had left me out, knowing how much I loved it here. But I understood. In those days, fathers left their property to their sons, not their daughters.

That's just how it was. Girls came second then, no matter how much they were loved. Nevertheless, that's the way my daddy wanted it, and it was his ranch. I can't go against my daddy's wishes. I just can't. I could never live with myself if I did."

J.R. had heard enough. His anger was boiling over. "I knew it! I was right all along! He's just like Digger Barnes, saying the Ewings stole everything from him! They all want to suck us dry, Momma—they want our land, and our money, and they won't stop till they've destroyed us! I knew he came back for some underhanded reason!"

"Let's leave the Barneses out of this one, shall we, J.R.?" Bobby suggested, trying to calm his brother down.

"Well, they were best friends, weren't they?" J.R. retorted.

Jock rose to put a stop to it. Shouting for the two of them to pipe down, his booming voice silenced them in a moment.

"Now, Miss Ellie," he said, turning his own anger toward his rebellious wife, "that's the end of the discussion. Southfork is ours, and that's the way it's gonna stay." He moved to leave the room, but Ellie's voice stopped him.

"It's not the end of the discussion, Jock," she said firmly.

"Don't get out of line, Ellie," he warned her. "Remember your place!"

Miss Ellie rose, flushed with fury. "What do you mean by that, Jock Ewing! What do you mean, my place?"

"I mean," her husband shouted, his face reddening, "that you are not in charge of this ranch, or our family businesses, and you are not the one to decide what's kept or given away around here! That's *my* place and always will be! I'm still the boss around here, whether you like it or not!"

The air was vibrating with tension. J.R. and Bobby had never seen their parents fight like this, screaming at each other at the top of their lungs.

Just then, Ellie put a stop to the argument, saying that whether Jock liked it or not, she had invited Garrison and his lady friend to lunch the next day. Then she stormed out, slamming the door behind her as hard as she could.

Jock turned to look at each of his boys in turn, tried to sputter some passing remark, failed, and then strode off in search of Miss Ellie, or a breath of night air, or a solitary double bourbon in the living room. He, too, slammed the door behind him.

J.R. and Bobby watched the objects on the shelves rattle from the vibration of the impact. Then they turned to face each other, a little embarrassed at the scene they had just witnessed, but even more concerned about the prospect of losing Southfork for good.

J.R. was still fuming. It was that girl, that floozy, Cathy—he was sure of it. Roping the old man with flattery and sex and then convincing him to come back here to steal their home from them! He said as much to Bobby, the whole idea galling him. Miss Ellie was right, it was never too late to right a wrong, and he vowed to himself to remember her words when the time was right.

Bobby tried to calm him down with the thought that perhaps Garrison wasn't after the ranch at all and wouldn't be interested in getting it back in any case. He suggested they talk to the old man before they got upset about everything.

J.R. merely snorted derisively. He knew better than that. An old man who's been bumming around the world all his life doesn't just show up at his ancestral hearth with a pretty young girl on his arm just to say hello!

"Pretty women have a way of running their men—you of all people, Bobby, ought to know that's true." And with that, he left Bobby not knowing whether to punch the wall or curse.

The next day was one of those warm, breezy, sunny days that come so often to Texas in the fall. It was a perfect day to be outdoors, and with that in mind, Miss Ellie had instructed Teresa to set a buffet lunch out on the patio.

She had ordered candied yams, remembering that they were a favorite of her brother's. Indeed, all night long, Ellie had searched her memories for Garrison's preferences, his old possessions that might still be lying around. She wanted to provide a bridge between past and present that he could cross over to begin a new life at Southfork. She watched as Teresa put the yams in the warmer, and then turned to greet

Lucy, who was approaching, loaded down with a stack of old seventy-eight records, which reached up to her chin.

"They were right up in the attic, just like you said, Grandma! Geez, look at all these . . . I've never heard of any of them."

"Well, that's good, Lucy," Miss Ellie said with a laugh. "You'll have to do some getting acquainted with the old tunes. Those were your Uncle Garrison's before he went away. I hope they're still in good condition. Why don't you go inside and try them out?"

Lucy departed, excited by the prospect of hearing all the corny old songs, and Ellie, feeling quite pleased with herself, turned her attention back to the food.

Over by the pool, not far away, where Miss Ellie could see but not hear them, Bobby and Pam were sitting in adjacent beach chairs reading the Sunday paper. Or, to be more precise, Pam was reading. Bobby was staring at the paper, trying to concentrate, not on the front-page story, but on his feelings. He couldn't bear to look around him at the ranch that had been his home, but soon was to be his no longer.

Pam noticed him burying his nose in the paper, and knew right away what was bothering him. He had kept her up late the night before agonizing over it. She leaned over and touched his hair, and told him the same thing she had told him last night.

"Bobby, why don't you do what you said J.R.

ought to do, and wait and see whether Garrison really does want the ranch? Worrying about it beforehand isn't going to change anything, it's just going to upset you unnecessarily."

"It's not only the ranch, Pam," he answered, looking up. "Last night was the first time I ever saw my mother and my father really yell at each other. It's true they've had blowups before, but nothing like this one. Momma used to tell me about the old days, before I was born, when she and Daddy used to have big fights all the time. That's what this one reminded me of. It was as if . . . as if their whole relationship were on the line. Know what I mean? As if those forty years together didn't mean anything next to what they were fighting about. It was frightening, I'll tell you. That must be how my daddy used to fight with Grandpa Southworth over the ranch."

Pam could see that her husband was deeply troubled, but somehow, the prospect of the Ewings losing Southfork just left her unmoved. Perhaps it was because in her heart, she would have loved for the two of them to have a home of their own, away from his family and their tremendously powerful personalities. And as for Ellie and Jock blowing up at each other, she felt saddened about it, but it was good to see Miss Ellie standing up to her husband. Pam wanted to feel that she would do the same thing if the circumstances ever called for it. Still, Pam felt bad for her husband. She reached over and kissed him on the forehead. From the house could be heard the strains of a big band orchestra playing "Happy Days Are Here Again." She wondered if they really were . . .

J.R. was just coming down the stairs when he heard the music. He burst straight into the den, where Lucy was standing in front of the stereo, leafing through the stacks of records.

"Turn that contraption off, Lucy."

"I like the oldies but goodies, J.R.—what's the matter with you? Get up on the wrong side of bed this morning?"

J.R. was not amused. "You just do as I say, young lady, or you'll regret it, and you know I mean that."

He was not fooling around. Feeling like she wanted to strangle him, Lucy abruptly turned off the stereo and marched out of the room.

As soon as she was gone, J.R. moved over to the desk and picked up the phone. When a secretary answered, he said, "This is J.R. Ewing speaking. Put me on with Dan Marsh, please."

On came the gravelly voice of the private investigator. "Hi, Mr. Ewing. Workin' on it," he said.

"How's it goin', Dan? Found any skeletons yet?"

There was a slight pause on the other end of the line. "So far, he's clean as a whistle. Has some bank accounts in Europe, but we can't find out how much he's got till tomorrow when the banks open up again. I can tell you this, though. Garrison Southworth's been around. Part of the problem is, he never stays in one place very long. Makes it hard to get anything on him."

J.R. scowled. "All right, Dan, I know you're doin' your best. Keep me posted, would you?"

J.R. hung up. He was not pleased. He had hoped to hit pay dirt quickly. This was obviously going to be more difficult than he had thought.

Soon afterward, Cathy and Garrison arrived, riding in a rented mid-size Chevrolet.

Nothing fancy, J.R. noted to Jock as they stood watching from the patio, sipping drinks that Teresa had brought them. J.R. mentioned to Jock that Garrison was the possessor of some European investments, and that he was working on finding out more about them. Sue Ellen looked on nearby.

Garrison emerged, and going straight over to Ellie, embraced her. Then he introduced her to Cathy Baker, who had come up behind him.

"So this is the famous Ellie Southworth Ewing," Cathy greeted, smiling. "I must say Garrison speaks very highly of you—in fact, he hasn't stopped talking about you for months!"

Ellie, for her part, seemed pleased to meet Cathy as well. "So you're the one who convinced Garrison to finally come home. I'm so grateful to you."

Garrison, noticing that the rest of the family were hanging back, said, "You seem to be alone in your gratitude."

But Ellie ignored him, saying only that the two of them needed to settle some business together, but first, she wanted Cathy to meet the family.

She led them up to the patio just as Bobby and Pam were emerging from the pool. Jock, J.R. and Sue Ellen, seeing the newcomers, moved slowly toward them. Jock was already feeling sorry that he'd allowed Miss Ellie to finally talk him out of lunching at the club.

"Everybody, this is Cathy Baker," said Miss Ellie. "Cathy, you'll have plenty of time to get to know everybody over lunch—we're having a buffet out here on the patio." She pointed to the food warmers in the corner.

Bobby, having met Cathy once before, came up to her first. "Welcome back, Cathy—nice to see you again." They shook hands, polite if not exactly warm.

Then J.R. moved forward as Teresa arrived with drinks for the newcomers.

"Miss Baker, is it?" J.R. asked, extending his hand and smiling his warmest welcoming smile. "Glad to know you. Have you ever been to Dallas before, ma'am?"

"Why, no, I haven't," Cathy admitted.

"In that case, how would it be if you and I took a short little tour around the ranch—just for a few minutes. I'll have you back in plenty of time for lunch. What do you say?"

Cathy smiled. "I say that'd be just fine. . . ." She paused, not knowing his name.

"Call me J.R.," he said.

"J.R.," she repeated.

Then the two of them walked off toward J.R.'s 280 SE as he pointed out landmarks left and right.

Bobby looked after them, deeply troubled. He

knew what J.R. was up to, and he didn't like it. No, he didn't like it at all.

Having shown her a few choice spots around the ranch, all the while asking her as obliquely as he could about her past, her relationship with Garrison, and his financial situation, he had learned virtually nothing. Her responses were as guarded as his questions. Eventually he led her on a tour of the stables, which were only a hundred yards or so from the ranch house, and the last stop on their little tour.

"It's so big," she wondered at it as they walked along. "I never realized that a ranch could be so huge!"

J.R. laughed in mock humility. "Oh, I only showed you a small corner of it. You'd need your sleeping bag if you intended to ride from one side to the other!"

She smiled at his typical Texas response. It was a lovely ranch, though. "It's not surprising that Garrison missed it so much," she mused.

"Oh? I thought it was you who convinced him to come back." J.R. thought he'd finally found his opening.

"I don't understand," she said.

"Let me make it a little plainer for you," he obliged. "Here's an old man, hasn't been home for forty years, and all of a sudden he meets a young lady and decides all on his own to come back?"

She stared hard at him, not wanting to believe he was insinuating what she thought he was insinuating. "I still don't understand," she said.

"Coming back home was very important to Garrison. The most important thing in his life right now."

J.R. saw that he would have to twist a little harder to get the top off the bottle. "Have you two set the date for the wedding yet?" he asked offhandedly.

"Wedding? Oh, no, we have no plans to get married . . . not at all. Is that how it looks to—well, I suppose I can see how it might look that way."

He had her. He could tell. "Don't give me that," he barked, pressing his advantage. "Let's talk turkey here, Miss Baker. You've cooked up a nice little plan, but you can't fool me—I'm a schemer from way back. You're gonna marry a nice old man who's gonna leave you a big Texas ranch, am I right?"

Cathy gasped as though she'd been punched in the gut. The depths to which this man had suddenly sunk stunned her, throwing her completely off guard. How could this man and Garrison be from the same family?

"That's an absolutely outrageous accusation!" she defended herself, furious.

"Oh, come on now!" He smiled, feeling he had hit pay dirt. "Don't try to tell me you're with that old mastodon just 'cause you're in love with him! Don't make me laugh!"

She almost spat at him, just barely managing to restrain herself. "I find you nauseating," she said as she spun on her heels and stormed back toward the house.

J.R. stared after her, still smiling as he

watched her luscious figure retreat into the after-noon sun.

"Nonsense," he said to himself. "I'm sure you're far from nauseated. In fact, young lady, as one schemer to another, I'll bet that if we weren't up against each other, we could have gone for each other in a big, big way."

Ellie, after the introductions were complete, took a walk of her own, leading Garrison away from the house to the site of the old ranch house, about a quarter of a mile away. There she sat him down and told him of her plan.

The old man was plainly touched and, in spite of his hard exterior, could not keep himself from shedding a few silent tears. He was astounded that his sister would make such a monumental move for him, especially after the way he had abandoned her all those years ago. She was truly a grand woman, her father's daughter, and she was carrying out what she perceived to be her father's wishes.

Silently, deeply moved, he walked back with her to the patio, where the others were waiting. They knew, of course, why Ellie had drawn him away, and Garrison could tell that they knew.

As they returned, Jock was the first to approach Garrison. "I just have to say," he said, frowning, "that I'm opposed to Miss Ellie's plans. Firmly opposed."

Garrison nodded. "I'm not surprised you feel that way," he said simply.

Bobby stepped up and asked his uncle what he planned to do in light of Miss Ellie's offer.

Garrison thought for a moment, and was about to reply when Cathy came running up, fresh from her encounter with J.R.

They all clustered around her, and Garrison asked her what had upset her so. It was obvious that something was the matter, but she insisted that she was all right and absolutely refused to say what had transpired between her and J.R. They would never have gotten the story, either, but at that moment J.R. himself ambled up to the patio and spelled it out for them.

"The reason Miss Baker is so upset is that I exposed her dirty little scheme for her. The jig is up, Uncle Garrison."

Garrison's face grew beet red with anger. How dare this fellow insult Cathy! And right in front of his eyes, too!

"What do you mean, her dirty little scheme?" It was more a warning than a question.

Ellie rushed to put herself between them in an effort to avoid the storm that was about to break. Her efforts, however, were too little and too late.

"Get out of my way, Ellie," shouted her brother. "I want your son, your firstborn Ewing son, to tell me for himself just what he meant by that black little insinuation he just made! Go ahead, J.R. Ewing—tell us all what scheme you mean!"

J.R. was happy to oblige, but in his own way. In J.R.'s world, offense was always the best defense, and this argument was no exception.

"I think you're the one who ought to do the

telling, Uncle Garrison. Why don't you tell everybody how you came to pick out a pretty young girl to be your wife . . . and at your age, too! How'd you get her, Uncle Garrison? Surely not through physical attraction! No, it's only money that draws young beauties to old barnacles like you! So you tell her you've got family back in Texas, and there's a big old ranch there that really belongs to you! So you bring her back here, see if you can't manipulate your kind-hearted sister into giving you back what you forfeited by your actions forty years ago!"

Speechless, Garrison could only look at his antagonist. "Why, you are a chip off the old Ewing block, aren't you, J.R.! You sure raised this boy right, Jock! Right into the sewer! He opens his mouth and filthy lucre flows out instead of words! He's nothing but a heartless money machine, grinding out the bucks and grinding up the poor helpless people who get in his way! Yessir, a Ewing through and through!"

"He's just telling the truth as he sees it," Jock said in his son's defense. "I'd say he's pretty near the mark."

J.R., seeing that his father approved of what he'd said, went even further. "If you insist on trying to get Southfork away from us, we'll just have to take you to court. And believe me, Uncle Garrison, we've got enough money to outlast you in the legal system, no matter how much you've got salted away in those Swiss banks of yours!"

Garrison's hands were clenched into tight fists, but he held them at his sides. His dander was up, all right, but not for a physical brawl. In a perverse way, it made him happy that he was involved in a fight with the Ewings. It made his blood flow quicker, heightened his sense of purpose.

"Good!" he shouted. "The Southworths versus the Ewings! You may think that might always makes right, but let me tell you something —Garrison Southworth is not poor old Digger Barnes. No sir! We Southworths are a strong breed. We don't roll over and die, or sink into a whiskey bottle. You are in for the fight of your lives!" And grabbing Cathy, he stormed off toward his car.

Horrified, Miss Ellie screamed after him to wait. He turned to her, his face red with anger.

"Ellie, you married him. You made your own bed, and now you've got to lie in it. But I don't, and I won't!" With that, he and Cathy were off in a cloud of dust.

Stunned, Miss Ellie stumbled back toward the others. She walked right up to J.R. and screamed in his face.

"How dare you! You've got your nerve, talking to my brother like that! It's unforgivable, J.R. You may be the boss of Ewing Oil, but you're not the boss around here—and you're certainly not *my* boss!"

Her rage boiling over, she turned and ran crying into the house.

J.R. turned apologetically to his father, as if to

say, "I'm sorry, Daddy, that Momma's so upset, but I did what I had to do."

Jock just looked at him, cold as ice, agreeing with his son, but furious with him at the same time. The rest of the family looked on, not knowing what to say.

Chapter Five

Bobby had seen all he cared to see. Making some excuse or other, he went upstairs to his and Pam's bedroom alone. There he showered after his swim in the pool and began dressing. By the time Pam got upstairs, he was dressed and was just putting on his jacket to go out.

Pam was not used to seeing her husband so agitated, although she could certainly understand his mood. Bobby Ewing, like his mother, put family ties above all else, and one member of the family had been offended by another. Bobby, the peacemaker, was going into action, and Pam guessed at what he was about to do.

"Going to see Garrison?" she asked.

He nodded. "I'm going to try and see if I can't smooth some ruffled feathers."

Pam suddenly realized that he would have left without telling her if she hadn't happened to come into the bedroom when she did. The previous day she had admitted to not caring very much about the loss of Southfork, and now she felt guilty that she hadn't stood more firmly behind Bobby.

"Wait for me," she said, hurrying to change. "I won't be but a minute."

They arrived at Garrison's hotel suite about an hour later. All the way there in the car they planned how they would go about dealing with the old man's anger, how they would explain away what J.R. had said. But when they got there, it was not Garrison, but Cathy, who opened the door to them.

"All right," she agreed when they asked if they could come in, "but try to speak softly. He's just fallen asleep."

"Fallen asleep?" Pam said, surprised. "Does he usually take an afternoon nap?"

"Well, no, not usually, but lately . . ." Cathy answered. "After what happened out at the ranch, I thought I'd never get him to calm down enough to sleep, but I finally managed it. I don't blame him for being upset—that happens sometimes in the anger phase, but I should have gotten him out of there sooner, as soon as I knew which way the wind was blowing. It was very unprofessional of me to go off with J.R. like that and leave him alone for so long."

Bobby and Pam looked at each other, perplexed. Anger phase? Unprofessional? What was she talking about?

Cathy noticed their confusion and hastened to enlighten them. "You see, contrary to what you all seem to believe, Garrison and I are not romantically involved. He's my patient, and I'm his nurse."

Bobby and Pam were speechless. How could they and the family have been so wrong?

"But why a nurse round the clock like this?" Bobby finally managed to say. "He seems healthy as a horse."

Cathy thought for a moment silently. "I'm not supposed to let on," she said. "He gave strict orders about that. But in light of what happened today, and of Miss Ellie's plans to give Garrison the ranch, I think she—and you—ought to know."

She fell silent again, gathering herself for what she was about to say. Pam interrupted her, trying to bring her back into conversation.

"You were talking about the anger phase . . ." she prompted.

"Yes, that's what's going on in his mind right now. He blows up at the least little thing. There's no reason for his outbursts—this afternoon excepted. It's all very normal under the circumstances. I'm a specialist in dealing with these types of cases, you see, and it happens to most of my patients. First there's the denial, then the anger, and finally, one hopes, acceptance."

Bobby gulped. "Acceptance?"

"That's right," Cathy affirmed. "Acceptance of death."

The two visitors gasped in horror.

"Yes," Cathy went on, looking them straight in the eye. "Your uncle has come home, not to take Southfork from you, but to die in the bosom of his family."

Dinner came and went, but Bobby and Pam said nothing about what they had learned. The meal was somber, with everybody angry at everybody else, or so it seemed. No one had the temerity to be cheerful, and a black pall hung over the dining room, each of the Ewings thinking their separate sad or angry or hurt thoughts.

Later, when Bobby and Pam had excused themselves and had gone up to their room, they lay under the covers in the dark, staring at the moonlight that poured in through the window. She asked him why he had chosen not to say anything to the family at dinner, or at least to Miss Ellie.

Bobby had to confess that all night long, whenever he had looked at his mother, his courage had failed him. He couldn't bear to cause her so much additional pain after all the hurt she had undergone that afternoon at the hands of J.R. and Jock. Besides, J.R. and Jock had been sitting right there, their moods blacker than crude oil.

"I kept waiting for the right time, but it never came," he lamented.

"Bad news is never easy to break to people, Bobby," she counseled him. "When do you think *would* be the right time?"

"Never, of course. You're right," he admitted, "but listen, should I really be the one to tell her? Why not Garrison himself? How can I tell her that she's about to lose her brother again, so soon after finding him? I don't think I have it in me, Pam, I really don't."

"Think of Miss Ellie, Bobby, not of yourself. She needs to know! She would want to know, don't you agree?"

There was no denying it: Pam was right. And if he waited for the right time, he'd be waiting until Garrison was dead and buried.

It was early Monday morning, but in Switzerland the banks had long been open. J.R. sat on his bed. He was fully dressed and ready for work, the telephone in his hand, while Sue Ellen sat at her vanity, putting the finishing touches on her makeup.

"Yeah, Marsh," J.R. was saying, "that's the kind of information I expected to get. Right. The check will be in the mail today. Good work, boy, I appreciate it. Bye."

Turning to his wife, a satisfied smile on his face, he said, "Well, Sue Ellen, old J.R. is never wrong about things like this. The old man had—and I say *had*—sixty-five thousand socked away in Swiss banks. Drew it all out in the last few months. I'll give you three guesses where it all went!"

Sue Ellen smirked into the mirror. "Good old Cathy Baker, no doubt. Like most kept women, she must have expensive tastes. Isn't that right, J.R.?"

Her husband ignored the innuendo, concentrating on the matter at hand.

"Sixty-five thousand must be running out. I'll

bet that's why they showed up at the ranch just now."

Sue Ellen began to worry again. Southfork had come to mean a lot to her. Also it was her unborn child's inheritance, and she worried every time she thought something might take it away. Finally, the thought of Cathy Baker as a rich widow living at Southfork, while Sue Ellen had to inhabit smaller quarters, was more than she could bear.

"They can't get the ranch legally, can they?" she asked again.

"Don't worry about a thing, darlin'," J.R. reassured her. "Even if the law is on their side, we can make it so expensive for them in court procedures that they'll just have to give up after a while."

"Yes, I suppose you can," she said. "But what if Miss Ellie insists on giving it to him?"

J.R. laughed a mirthless little laugh. "Don't you worry about Momma," he said flatly. "Daddy'll talk her out of it, you wait and see."

Just at that moment, Ellie was sitting on the patio, alone, drinking the coffee that Raoul had brought out to her. She had been there for some time, absorbed in her thoughts.

It pained her to be at war with her own family, but if there was ever a good cause for that kind of war, it was the cause of one's own conscience. Ellie knew that what she was doing was right, was the only right way to proceed, and she intended to do just that, in spite of any arguments her family might put forward. Nevertheless, her resolve didn't make her feel any better about things.

Bobby knew she was on the patio. He had seen her from his bedroom window. Now, sensing that the time was as right as it was ever going to be, he came downstairs, knowing full well that they would not be intruded upon. Both Jock and J.R. were still as determined as ever to fight Miss Ellie, and under the circumstances, they would try to stay far away from her for the moment.

Her back was toward him, and she didn't hear him approaching until he was right next to her. He bent down and kissed his mother on the forehead.

She reached up and stroked his cheek. Her good boy, Bobby. How she loved him. She asked him to sit down and have a cup of coffee with her. Normally, on Monday morning he was on his way to somewhere or other, but it didn't occur to her that it was anything unusual for him to sit leisurely down with her at 9:00.

"I guess at least you and I are on speaking terms, aren't we?" she said sadly.

"That's over with, Momma. I have to tell you something. Something I found out yesterday that changes everything."

Misunderstanding him, she begged him not to find fault with her decision for yet other reasons; she had had enough fighting.

He shook off her warning. "It's about Uncle Garrison—Pam and I went to visit him at his hotel yesterday, after the fight."

Miss Ellie sat bolt upright, momentarily upset.

"Oh!" she cried in surprise. "You didn't argue with him, I hope! You didn't try to talk him out of it, did you?"

"No, Momma," he assured her. "It's nothing like that. In fact, we didn't even speak to Garrison while we were there. He was taking an afternoon nap, so we only spoke to Cathy. That's what I want to tell you about."

Miss Ellie tried to understand what her son was saying. "Are you going to try to tell me that she is a little gold digger after all, just like J.R. said she was? Because if you are—"

"No, Momma, that's just it," he said, putting his hand on her arm. "Cathy Baker is not a little gold digger. She's a specially trained nurse who deals with the terminally ill. She's working full-time for Uncle Garrison. He's dying, Momma."

In the hotel suite, Garrison and Cathy were having breakfast catered by room service. Their table was positioned in front of the window where they could look out over the whole of downtown Dallas as it awoke to Monday morning.

The fight of the previous day had exhausted Garrison, and he had slept all through the afternoon and night, waking only after the sun was up. He looked much better, more rested, and his fighting spirit had returned.

"Damn them!" he was shouting, waving his fork and knife over his eggs as he spoke. "They think they can get away with anything just because they're rich and powerful! And they always have gotten away with it, too—but not this time. I've got nothing to lose, Cathy, and I'm going to fight them to my dying breath!"

Cathy answered in level tones, not getting drawn into his fury. "Your dying breath may come sooner than a legal judgment, Garrison."

"Be quiet!" he yelled, smashing his fists down on the table. "If you can't say anything supportive, then dammit, don't say anything at all!"

"I am being supportive, Garrison. I'm telling you what you need to hear—the truth."

"By God, isn't that peachy?" he said sarcastically. "Well, as far as I'm concerned, from now on, you have a license to lie to me, all right? Because I've heard enough truth in the last six months for one lifetime."

Just then a knock sounded on the door. Cathy rose to answer it as she and Garrison exchanged a wary look between them. But it was only Miss Ellie who had come, not Jock or J.R., or one of their lawyers.

Cathy escorted her into the dining area, and then excused herself, leaving the two of them alone. From the look on Miss Ellie's face, she could tell that Bobby had passed his information on to his mother.

Garrison rose to greet her, pleased that she had come in spite of what must have been a lot of flak from her family.

"Aren't you afraid I'll corrupt you with my grasping intentions, Ellie? I'm surprised they didn't hog-tie you at home to keep you from seeing me!"

Ellie's eyes were misted over with tears, but Garrison, seeing them, misunderstood their reason. He thought they came from the pain caused by hearing the bitter truth.

"Don't be angry at me, Garrison. You have no reason," she pleaded with him.

"Making a home with Jock Ewing is reason enough, Ellie."

"You don't really understand Jock, Garrison," Ellie said, defending her husband and her marriage. "You don't understand him, or his sons, and I don't know whether you ever will."

Garrison's face flushed hot and red. "I haven't forgotten the way that husband of yours destroyed my friend Digger Barnes. Jock and that son of his would like to treat me the very same way, but I'm not going to roll over for them. Not me! I'm going to give them the fight of their lives before I'm through!"

"Garrison, you're so angry! So angry all the time!" Miss Ellie's gaze searched his face. "But it's not Jock or J.R. that you're angry at. Is it? It's nothing human . . . what you're angry at, is it, Garrison? Nothing you can fight, even if you want to. I'm right, aren't I?"

He spun away from her, waving his hands in the air as if warding off some unwanted truth.

"You don't know what you're talking about!" he screamed at her. "You don't know anything!"

Miss Ellie remained calm. "Garrison," she said softly, "there's something you have to face. We all face it sooner or later, and nobody wants to do it by themselves. Let me face it with you. Please. I want to be there with you."

He stopped, stunned by the realization that she had somehow seen through his bluster.

"Ellie . . . I don't want the ranch . . . and you're right . . . I shouldn't be wasting my time fighting Jock and J.R. I didn't come back to cause you pain—please believe that. I never wanted to hurt you or shake up your life. I just wanted to see you again . . . to see our home again."

He paused to sniff and wipe his eyes with his forearm. "I'll go back to Europe tomorrow . . . today, this afternoon. I'll just go back. . . ."

"Garrison," she said, looking up into his eyes, "you can't run away! You can't flee from life like that!"

"*No!*" he wailed, clenching and unclenching his fists. "It's not life I'm fleeing from, Ellie! I've never run from life! It's . . . it's death . . ."

Ellie held his head in her arms as he sank to his knees with the realization. It was the first time since his diagnosis that he had uttered the word—death. Reality. Truth. Death. He had said it, and he knew it was real.

"I'm going to die, Ellie," he whispered. "I'm going to die. . . ."

They held each other close, their tears mingling in a flood of release.

Ray had not heard from his roughneck friend Matt since their visit, and lately he had begun to think that he would get nowhere with his search efforts. But when that Monday morning Matt called him, saying he wanted to meet him at the bar for lunch, the same bar they'd met in before.

Ray got there first and was working on a beer when he saw the burly oil worker enter the place and walk over to him.

"Ray," he said, sitting down and ordering a beer, "I think we hit pay dirt."

"Great!" said Ray, sitting up. "What's the good news?"

"Well, there's a guy I dug up who was doin' some work out on Southfork a few weeks ago. I told him to meet us here, should be here any minute. He might be willing to spill the beans, if there are any beans to spill. Got the feeling he might want something for his trouble, though . . ."

"Don't worry," Ray said, patting his pocket, "I've got enough here to make him happy. What's his name?"

"Charlie Waters," Matt said, looking at his watch. "Geez, he ought to be here by now . . ."

At that very moment, Charlie Waters strode into the offices of Ewing Oil and asked Louella if he could speak to J.R. Ewing. Normally J.R. would not have seen a roughneck in his office, but it was a quiet Monday, and, seeing that Waters had told Louella to tell him it was important, he gave orders that Charlie be shown in.

J.R. rose to greet him. He flattered himself that he had the common touch, that he knew how to talk to the little people, and he stretched out his hand to shake that of the slimy-looking oil worker, reminding himself to wash up afterward.

"What seems to be the trouble, Mr. Waters? Anything I can help you with?"

Waters shuffled a bit, a grin emerging on one side of his mouth. "I think I might be the one who's able to help you, Mr. Ewing," he drawled.

J.R. walked out from behind his desk, smiling now in anticipation. "And what might this little tidbit of information be?" he asked in conspiratorial tones.

"Well," answered the grinning roughneck, "there was a cowboy snoopin' around, goin' into all the oil worker's bars, trying to dig up what happened that night out at Southfork when we tested the old boarded up well . . . I was there that night, and I heard he was lookin' to speak to me. But I figured you might want to know about it first, and that's why I came to you."

J.R.'s eyes widened. His face showed all his pleasure with Charlie Waters, but none of his fury at Ray Krebbs.

"Is that right, now?" he said, slapping Charlie on the back and moving over to the bar, where he offered his guest a stiff drink. "Well, isn't that something, now. Mr. Waters, you're a very bright individual, and it was good thinking on your part to come to me first . . . yessir, I think you're going to find that you made the right choice. I'm gonna see to it that you're well rewarded, sir, for making that right choice. *Well* rewarded!"

With that he laughed his wicked laugh, toasting his guest and his good fortune.

* * *

That afternoon, upon her return from her visit with Garrison, Ellie directed Bobby to invite the family into the living room, saying that she wanted to speak to them about something important. The whole gathering had a very official, diplomatic flavor to it, due to the ongoing fight within the family.

She sat there alone until Bobby returned.

"They should all be down in a couple of minutes, Momma," he said. "And Pam's on her way back from The Store. She ought to get here anytime, too."

Miss Ellie thanked him and settled back to wait.

In a few moments, J.R. and Sue Ellen came downstairs. He had come back early to speak to Ray, taking half the day off from the office solely in order to put a stop to that cowboy's meddling. He had given him a royal piece of his mind when Ray had admitted to pursuing the matter of Section 40, but J.R. had not let on that he was involved in any way. Ray might suspect whatever he chose to, so long as there was no proof.

Miss Ellie directed them to sit down and await the others. She was not going to begin until they were all present.

Lucy was next, flying in from outside, wondering what could be the matter. This kind of event was extremely rare at Southfork, where the family gathered formally only for meals, and even then, rarely for lunch. Ellie refused to explain, only directing Lucy to her seat until Jock arrived.

Pam burst in the door at that moment and hurried to her husband's side. They sat down together on the sofa.

Now Jock appeared, having cleaned himself off from working outdoors. He remained lingering in the doorway. Obviously, he was still steaming. J.R. had not yet had time to tell him about Garrison's investments.

"What do you want, Ellie?" he asked gruffly. "I'm busy out there."

No one had ever heard Jock talk to Miss Ellie that way. She gently told him to sit down, but he refused, preferring to listen from where he was. Now it remained only for Miss Ellie to speak her piece.

"I want you all to know that I've invited Garrison to come live here with us at Southfork."

The explosion was immediate. "No way, Ellie," Jock said, his eyes burning coals. "If he's movin' in, then I'm movin' out! I'm not gonna live with that man, no matter what you say."

Miss Ellie sighed. "He isn't going to be with us for very long," she said softly.

This remark took Jock aback. "What is that supposed to mean?" he asked curtly.

"It means," his wife answered, "that although you may not want to accept it as the truth, my brother Garrison is not a gold digger, and neither is Cathy Baker. Not everyone in the world is as devious as you believe. Not everyone is greedy and soulless."

"You mean, like we are, isn't that right?" It was J.R.'s turn to talk. "Momma, I can understand you bein' upset, but if you're trying to tell us that Uncle Garrison came back just to see you and for no other reason, you're just a victim of that man's mendacity. He's a liar, Momma. I had a detective look into it."

Bobby moved to restrain his brother from going any further, but Miss Ellie waved him off. "J.R.," she asked, "then this detective of yours must also have told you that Garrison is about to die?"

From the doorway, Jock shook himself to attention. Suddenly he understood everything and felt greatly ashamed and sorry for his conduct.

"Garrison came back to die at home, in the bosom of his family," continued Miss Ellie. "Cathy Baker is his specially trained nurse, and from what she says, Garrison has only a few days to live. And he's going to spend them here—with us."

Jock found that he was close to tears. The proportions of the human tragedy unfolding before him, together with what he now saw as his own base behavior, left him choked up and shaken.

"I'm truly sorry," he said, going to his wife. "I didn't know. How could any of us have known? Oh, Ellie, I'm so sorry."

"I forgive you, Jock," she said, throwing her arms around him for a moment. "I'm over my anger now, and so is Garrison. And I see now how much you've come to love the ranch. It's too bad it had to happen this way, that's all."

"He's surely welcome to come stay with us,

Ellie," said Jock hoarsely. "Bring him home. We'll be waiting."

Ellie nodded. She was going to do just that.

"Just one thing," she added. "Please, everyone, don't make a big thing out of this. Garrison just wants to be left alone to die in peace. No crying or anything like that, no farewells . . . just everyday, ordinary Southfork life—okay?"

She was about to cry herself, and, without waiting for them to promise, she hurried out of the room.

Jock cast a glum look at J.R. and then turned to follow after his wife. He had some fence-mending to do.

Garrison and Cathy moved in the next morning. Things were spectacularly quiet and peaceful, and Garrison, too, felt at peace. Now that he had come to accept his own imminent death, he seemed willing to leave the cares of this world to those who would be hanging around a while longer than he would. He didn't make much of the apologies he received from Jock and J.R., and he didn't spend much time with any of them except at dinner.

Only with Miss Ellie did he spend any considerable length of time. That first afternoon, as they walked the ranch together, Garrison felt the land becoming a part of him again, as he would soon become a part of it again. Every tree, every blade of grass, the smells of the horses and the cattle, the feel of them, all seemed to mingle with the fibers of his being. He felt whole again, for the first time since he had been a young man.

Soaps & Serials™ Fans!

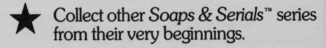 Order the *Soaps & Serials*™ books you have missed in this series.

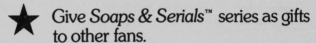 Collect other *Soaps & Serials*™ series from their very beginnings.

Give *Soaps & Serials*™ series as gifts to other fans.

...see other side for ordering information

Soaps & Serials™
From Pioneer Communications Network, Inc.

You can now order previous titles of *Soaps & Serials*™ Books by mail!

Just complete the order form, detach, and send together with your check or money order payable to:

Soaps & Serials™
120 Brighton Road, Box 5201
Clifton, NJ 07015-5201

Please <u>circle</u> the book #'s you wish to order:

The Young and The Restless	1	2	3	4	5	6	7	8
Days of Our Lives	1	2	3	4	5	6	7	8
Guiding Light	1	2	3	4	5	6	7	8
Another World	1	2	3	4	5	6	7	8
As The World Turns	1	2	3	4	5	6	7	8
Dallas™	1	2	3	4	5	6	7	8
Knots Landing™	1	2	3	4	5	6	7	8
Capitol™	1	2	3	4	NOT AVAILABLE			

Each book is $2.50 ($3.50 in Canada).

Total number of books
circled _____ × price above = $ _____

Sales tax (CT and NY residents only) $ _____

Shipping and Handling $ _____ .95

Total payment enclosed $ _____
(check or money orders only)

Name _____

Address _____ Apt# _____

City _____

State _____ Zip _____

Telephone (_____) _____
Area code

D 8

"I'm glad I came home," he confessed to her as they strolled through the stables.

Ellie smiled deeply at him. Her brother. He had come back to her after all, and everything else was unimportant. The moments they shared together now would be memories she could cherish for the rest of her life.

"I'm so happy you're here," she said, taking his hand as they emerged back into the sunlight.

"I never hated this place, you know," he said. "It was only that Daddy thought I was so inadequate. . . ."

Ellie stopped. "That's not true, Garrison! You're wrong about that!"

He turned to her and looked in her eyes pleadingly. Had the old man said so to her? he wanted to know.

"Not in so many words, Garrison—but he left you Southfork! Don't you see what he meant to do by that?"

Garrison stood there dumbstruck. It was true! His father had loved and respected him after all, in spite of all the harsh words between them. How he wished that they'd been able to share that love while the old man was still alive. Well, perhaps they'd soon be seeing each other again . . .

For now, and for the rest of his brief span in this sphere, what mattered most was that he was home with his family, and that he was at peace. He looked out over the breathtaking glory that was Southfork Ranch, knew that it belonged to him, but more, that he belonged to it. And he was blissfully happy. He could see himself as

God saw him, as a tiny figure on his knees in a vast, swaying sea of grass.

Garrison died ten days later. Up until his death, he seemed healthy and happy, although he did sleep away more and more of the day toward the end. Miss Ellie found him one morning, in his bed, his hands folded on his chest, and a smile on his face.

Cathy Baker had already left, having straightened Garrison's room before she went. She did not want to say good-bye, still remembering what had happened when she and Garrison had first arrived.

They buried him in the Southworth family plot, on the top of a low rise overlooking a lake on one of the more remote parts of the ranch. It was a simple ending, and nobody said much. The wounds of his reappearance were still healing when he left, but now Garrison was home for good and would never leave again.

Chapter Six

Just as things were getting back to normal around the ranch, a new problem surfaced, interrupting the Southfork routine. The crisis was precipitated by another new arrival from out of town—Sue Ellen's little sister, Kristin, and her mother, Mrs. Shepard. They hadn't come for a visit, either, as their letters had intimated—they had come for an indefinite period. Mrs. Shepard had even taken an apartment for the two of them, knowing as she did that neither Sue Ellen nor Miss Ellie would invite them to stay at Southfork.

Miss Ellie got along with almost everybody, and yet, she had always had a peculiar antipathy for Mrs. Shepard ever since she had known her. There was something about the woman—something so calculating, so heartless, and so bitter all at the same time, that it gave Miss Ellie the shivers just to be near her. She felt sorry for

Sue Ellen, who had had to live with Mrs. Shepard for twenty years without a father around to mitigate that woman's influence. Sue Ellen had turned out all right, in spite of some little quirks. It was a wonder she had not been totally ruined. Miss Ellie wondered if Kristin had turned out equally well.

For Sue Ellen's part, her mother's coming was a coin with two faces. On the good side, she and Kristin would be there to see her new baby when it arrived. But on the other, Sue Ellen's mother was not the person she wanted to be around right now.

Mrs. Shepard had devoted her life to finding the best possible matches for her daughters, and the crowning triumph of her life had been the day Sue Ellen had netted J.R. Ewing. And she would never understand the torment Sue Ellen had gone through being J.R. Ewing's wife. The constant infidelities, the coldness, the hardness, the loneliness . . . To Mrs. Shepard, the power and prestige that went with being a Ewing should have been more than enough to compensate. No, she would never understand how Sue Ellen had been driven into Cliff Barnes' arms. If she knew that Sue Ellen's baby was probably Cliff's, she would not have been at all pleased.

The day the Shepards arrived, Sue Ellen helped them move in and stayed for dinner and most of the evening. J.R. had not joined her. When he had heard that Sue Ellen's mother was coming, and coming to stay, he had hardly been thrilled. In spite of her extreme admiration for

J.R. Ewing, J.R. himself did not like his mother-in-law at all, and he had suddenly decided that he had to go to Austin on business for a few days. Sue Ellen realized that J.R. had wanted to avoid just the sort of obligation that Sue Ellen had felt on the night of their arrival.

It was a torturous day, and a worse evening. Sue Ellen could not talk about any of the things that mattered to her, not about her troubles with J.R., her love affair with Cliff, her uncertainty about the baby's parentage, her deepening doubts about the life she had made for herself. Her mother wanted only to talk about two things—the baby, and most of all, Kristin.

It seemed that the real reason Mrs. Shepard had come to Dallas was that Kristin was now, in her opinion, of marriageable age, and she wanted Sue Ellen to use her Ewing connections to help find Kristin a nice multimillionaire. It was all she talked about during one entire evening, and finally Sue Ellen practically ran from the house to avoid being harangued any further.

Now, the next morning, she sat in front of her vanity, putting the finishing touches on herself, admiring how well she looked. Her outfit, her makeup—everything was perfect—even her figure, which still showed no sign of her burgeoning pregnancy.

She was going into Fort Worth for a luncheon date with some ladies from her organization, the Daughters of the Alamo. Sue Ellen was a high-ranking officer in the group, and these particular ladies were also quite important. They had invited her out to Fort Worth to lunch at the new civic center, which they had helped to fund and were very proud of. It was a long way to travel, but it was important to impress these ladies, after all. They were her peers, the ones whose opinions counted as far as she was concerned. She was delighted and excited to go.

For a final dash of style, she took out the new designer scarf she had recently bought for herself but had not yet worn out of respect for Garrison's death. She felt that a decent interval had now passed. Sue Ellen considered herself an expert judge of etiquette, and no one would challenge her on that point. The scarf was stylish and unique—unmistakably her. She smiled as she wound it around her neck.

When she walked out onto the patio, most of the family had already finished breakfast and had departed, leaving only Miss Ellie behind. Ellie was still subdued and wan over her brother's death, but there was no grief as such. She had done everything she could for Garrison—he had died a happy man. And after all, seeing him again at all was something she had never imagined possible. It had been a short-lived gift from God, and her placidity now came from a certain sense of having been briefly blessed and then quickly returned to the ranks of ordinary humanity.

Seeing Sue Ellen, Ellie seemed to come to life, offering her juice and breakfast rolls, but Sue Ellen demurred, saying she still wasn't feeling quite like eating in the mornings.

The truth was, she was more concerned with keeping her weight down than with keeping her strength up. Being pregnant hadn't really sunk in on her yet. Oh, it had certainly given her more leverage with J.R., at least so far. And it was a big boost for her in her competition with Pam for the post of First Daughter of Southfork, raising her importance in Jock's and Ellie's eyes.

But what was on Sue Ellen's mind most, still, was her love affair with Cliff Barnes, terminated so artificially by her unexpected pregnancy. The knowledge that the baby was probably Cliff's made the separation even harder. Sue Ellen had had to choose between her rank and privileges, her opulent lifestyle, and Cliff. She had made her choice but was having trouble going along with it. She kept calling Cliff and trying to see him. Cliff, naturally, was pained by her continued presence in his life. It was hard enough for him to get over her without her coming around and calling him all the time. But she seemed unable to help herself. Although she probably was not aware of it, her concern for her figure most likely reflected her need to look good for Cliff so that they could continue seeing each other, ignoring the facts for just a little while longer.

The patio phone rang, and Sue Ellen stood up to answer it. It was Mrs. Shepard, calling to say how wonderful it had been to see Sue Ellen the night before, and how much she had missed seeing J.R. It was disgusting, thought Sue Ellen, the way her mother played up to J.R. For once, she had to sympathize with his desire to get out of a family obligation. His going to Austin on business was natural, given her mother's sudden arrival in town.

She promised her mother that when J.R. returned, he'd come over and say hello. But her mother was pushing for more. She wanted an invitation to Southfork for her and Kristin so that her younger daughter could meet some of Sue Ellen's friends. Eligible male friends. The woman never let up.

"When the time is right, Mother, I'll see that she meets some nice gentlemen," said Sue Ellen.

"Some very special and important nice gentlemen," her mother corrected her. "Not just anybody for my Kristin. You know how much I care about my girls."

Sue Ellen grimaced, thinking how much better her life might have been if her mother had cared a little less. She quickly said good-bye and hung up before she found herself saying something better left unsaid.

Cliff Barnes was at that very moment looking at his reflection in several mirrors as The Store's very expensive tailor fitted him for the first hand-tailored suit he had ever bought in his life.

Cliff, after his electoral defeat the November before, had decided to change his image—from idealistic loser to realistic winner. The underhanded tactics J.R. Ewing had used to keep him out of office had made him determined to do whatever it took to win, and image was a good place to start.

Pam stood by admiring him, smiling at the worried frown on Cliff's face. He was concerned that the suit look just right.

"Take it easy, Cliff," she joked. "You've got a long time to go till the next election!"

"Got to get an early start if you want to catch the worm," he replied, taking her comment seriously.

The tailor was finished. "It'll be ready the end of the week," he told his customer.

"Hey, it's only Tuesday!" Cliff complained. "Pammy, you work here . . . can't you pull a few strings for me? I'd like it a little sooner than that—tomorrow, say."

Pam told him she'd try. At least she would personally bring it over to his house when it was ready, saving him a trip. He hurriedly gave her a kiss, saying he was off to a meeting. Pam looked at the tailor and shrugged, shaking her head. Her brother had suddenly become a real go-getter.

Mary, Elizabeth and Carol, all members in good standing of the Daughters of the Alamo, sat at the lunch table with Sue Ellen, making small talk, chatting, and gossiping about other DOA members, who were, after all, the only people who really counted. They were very grateful and flattered that a person of Sue Ellen's standing in the organization had come all the way out to Fort Worth to lunch with them, and they talked a lot about the virtues of their fair city and its new civic center.

They looked around them at the luxuri-
ous surroundings—the new atrium, gleaming
chrome and glass everywhere—and were justly
proud. Sue Ellen, too, was impressed. They
had shown her the new hospital wing as well,
the one Sue Ellen's chapter of the DOA had
been so instrumental in raising funds for.
It had been instructive, but depressing, and
all four women were glad to escape to the civic center where things were so much more
pleasant.

Now the talk turned to Sue Ellen's pregnancy.
All three of the other ladies had children of their
own and husbands they loved to brag about. Sue
Ellen did an equal amount of bragging about
J.R., and wondered if these ladies were secretly
as unhappy with their husbands as she was with
hers. In fact, as they talked, Sue Ellen began to
get the feeling that they were probing into her
private life, trying to find the chinks that would
make her less enviable.

"Well," gushed Mary, "you certainly are doing
fine, Sue Ellen. When I was pregnant I had to
stay in bed for six months running—doctor's
orders!"

"J.R. must be just thrilled to death," cooed
Carol.

"Oh, yes," lied Sue Ellen. "He never stops
carrying on about it. He's gotten so affectionate
lately! He's always been a very loving husband,
but my goodness!"

Now the others knew Sue Ellen was lying.
J.R.'s philandering ways had long been the
source of juicy gossip, and his coldness toward

his wife was equally legend. Of course, not one of them would have dared confront Sue Ellen with the truth, but when she wasn't looking, the others exchanged knowing glances.

Sue Ellen, sensing that she wasn't being totally convincing, tried to change the subject, remarking how wonderful it was that her family had moved to Dallas to be near her. But the ladies weren't going to let her off the hook that easily.

"The way that J.R. loves his business!" said Elizabeth. "Why, honey, you've got to hog-tie him to his easy chair if you want him to spend some time with his child!"

Carol concurred. "My husband Charlie did a deal with him last year, and he said he'd never seen a man who loved his work the way J.R. did."

Sue Ellen caught the inferences. There was no mistaking their meaning. The good ladies were insinuating that J.R. loved his work more than he did Sue Ellen. So much more that Sue Ellen often came to DOA affairs unescorted. The ladies were, perhaps, also insinuating that the work J.R. was so devoted to wasn't just the oil business.

Sue Ellen flushed a bit. "J.R. is on a very important business trip to Austin right now, as a matter of fact—he's very conscientious about his responsibilities to the business. Yes, I'm very proud of my husband," she concluded, ending the discussion, and then proceeded to bury herself in the menu.

* * *

The Maxwell Building was one of the most imposing in Dallas, and Mr. Ben Maxwell was one of the city's movers and shakers. Cliff had called him after his recent election loss, asking for his financial help in the future, should he decide to run again. He was ready to take help where it was offered now, but still, he was somewhat surprised when Maxwell returned his call so soon.

Now, here he was, riding the elevator to the top floor, walking to the corner office for a meeting with Maxwell, at the other man's initiative. Cliff wondered what it could all mean . . .

In the office with Maxwell were two other men he'd met before, Emerson Ryder and Martin Smith. The three men represented a huge chunk of the Dallas building industry, and almost as large a chunk of the city's powerful elite.

Maxwell offered him coffee, and when he declined, got right down to business.

"Well, Mr. Barnes," he said in his oily, smooth voice, "you said you wanted our support. I must say we were surprised to hear from you. All during your campaign you were so insistent about keeping us at arm's length . . ."

"Well," Cliff explained, "I learned a lot last year. I learned that a man's platform doesn't mean much without the backing to go with it."

Maxwell agreed, sounding very sympathetic. "We still believe you are a worthy person, Mr. Barnes," he continued. "And if we've waited this long to speak with you, it was only that we were waiting for the right moment."

Cliff was confused, so Maxwell hastened to enlighten him.

"There is soon going to be a new Office of Land Management in our fair state. It will review all proposals for land use in the state —ranching, building, oil drilling . . ."

So they knew about his feud with J.R., Cliff thought to himself.

"The head of this office is going to be a very important and powerful man, and we feel that, what with your strong plank on ecology, you'd be ideal for the appointment."

An appointed position! No campaign and no election! No two-year wait! Power over J.R.! It was almost too good to be true.

"Are you sure I can have this job if I want it?" Cliff asked.

"That would be no problem," Maxwell assured him. "We're in a position to get you the appointment, and we're willing to do it."

Cliff was beginning to get very suspicious about all this. He didn't like Maxwell and his kind to begin with, and he didn't trust them. Why were they doing this for him?

"Just who do you mean by 'we,' sir?" he asked.

"Never mind that, Mr. Barnes." Maxwell brushed him off with a smile. "We want to help you, and that's all you need to know."

So . . . there was a catch after all. "I assume that you chose me for a reason . . ." Cliff prompted him. "Other than my good looks and charm, that is."

Maxwell smiled his shark's grin. "We believe

we can do business together," was his enigmatic reply.

"We can, if we happen to agree on a subject," Cliff cautioned him.

Maxwell momentarily lost his good humor. "I believe, Mr. Barnes, that we are the ones who are in the position to dictate that."

Cliff nodded, watching the smile return to Maxwell's face. That was the deal, then. The appointment in exchange for his soul, in exchange for the rubber stamp on whatever they wanted to do.

"I suppose you have a specific project in mind that you'd want me to approve for you," he said, feeling a headache coming on.

"Step right this way," said Maxwell, as if this were the cue he'd been waiting for all along.

He led Cliff over to the far corner of the room where a sheet covered a six-foot square object. As Maxwell lifted off the covering, Cliff could see that it was a handsomely rendered scale model of a very ambitious development. There, all in miniature, were apartment houses, shopping centers, office towers, even a few discreet factories dressed up to look modern and stylish.

Cliff was impressed. "What am I looking at?" he asked.

"This," said Maxwell proudly, "is what South Dallas will someday look like. Where you're standing is where downtown is, looking south."

Cliff was stunned. Maxwell was not talking about some scrubland, but about a development filled with houses and small businesses!

"Just what do you intend to do with all the people who live and work there right now?" he inquired, straining to be polite.

"Get rid of them," said Maxwell bluntly. "They're a bad element anyway. We don't want blight so near to downtown, do we?"

Cliff shuddered involuntarily. All those poor people, with no place to go . . .

"How will you get the land?" he wondered.

"Ever hear of the right of eminent domain? The land goes to the people who can do the most good for the general population. That's us." Maxwell folded his hands in front of him, waiting for Cliff's response.

So that was it, Cliff thought. The head of the Office of Land Management makes a few zoning changes, the houses get condemned, the people and businesses forced out, the new development is built, and the builders walk away with a quick couple of million in their pockets.

"Of course, we need your guarantee in advance that you'd approve our plans," said Maxwell in his ear.

"Of course," Cliff replied. So that was what they thought of him! That he was somebody who would sell his soul for power, somebody who would play dirty pool with the big boys and sell out the little people!

All his righteous anger welled up inside him, and he shook his head in disgust. He was willing to compromise with the dictates of political reality, but not to sell his soul altogether!

"I'm sorry, gentlemen," he said, trying to keep

his temper. "I'll do my best to forget everything you've said and shown me here. I'm out to be a realist, but not quite that kind of a realist." And with that, he quickly found the door and closed it behind him.

The three men looked darkly at each other after Cliff had left.

"Still the white knight, isn't he?" remarked Smith, not a little miffed.

"What say we forget about him and try someone a little more tractable, Ben?" said Ryder.

But Maxwell shook his head. Cliff Barnes had the credentials of an ecological crusader, a friend of the poor people, an incorruptible do-gooder. He was the perfect person for the job, and Maxwell knew how badly he wanted it.

"He'll come around, boys," he assured his cronies. "You wait and see."

Their luncheon over, the ladies headed across the civic center toward the garage where their cars were waiting. Sue Ellen was glad it was over. At times during the luncheon, she had felt that she was being grilled by the Spanish Inquisition. The way those ladies had inquired about J.R. and his devotion to business! She would have to speak to her husband when he returned from Austin. He was going to have to be faithful in future, she said to herself, and not only that, she was going to insist that he accompany her to more DOA functions, business or no business. Her activities mattered too, after all.

The civic center consisted of an atrium, con-

Chapter Seven

Steaming hot, Sue Ellen sat in front of her vanity, swinging one leg back and forth over the other like the pendulum of the doomsday clock. She was cooling her fury down with cold vodka. Her blood coursed hot inside her, and her temples were throbbing violently. Furious yet curiously detached, she awaited J.R.'s arrival.

She could hear the car drive up and the door open and close. She felt a rush as they ran headlong toward the confrontation, a battle that had been coming for seven years. She listened as his footsteps mounted the carpeted stairs and his hands turned the doorknob.

"Hello, darlin'," he said as he entered, not stopping to kiss her forehead, but going directly to the dressing table where he dropped his overnight bag. "Oh, now, darlin', do you think you ought to be drinking? Not good for the baby, is it?" he cautioned her, more disapproving than worried.

"You're right as usual, J.R.," she said evenly, draining the rest of her drink with a flourish. "Did you enjoy your trip?"

"Oh, it was about the same as always," he said noncommittally.

"You said a mouthful," she agreed sardonically. "First time I've ever gotten a straight answer to that question."

He stood still for a moment, wondering what she meant. Still not sure if she was on to him, he asked her what she was trying to say.

"I'm trying to say that you've been fooling around behind my back and lying about it. I'm trying to say I'm sick of it."

She could not have been plainer if she had tried. J.R. could see that there was going to be a frank discussion. He abandoned his breezy manner and bared his claws for battle.

"Is that right?" he challenged her.

"I was in Fort Worth today, J.R. At the civic center having lunch with some very important people. I had just spent a half an hour bragging about you, and telling them about your trip to Austin on 'business,' when you walked out of that bar with that hooker on your arm, smiling to beat the band."

J.R. sat on the bed and leaned over so his face was close to hers. He kept his voice low as he spoke, not wanting to alert the rest of the family to their fight.

"That lady was no hooker, Sue Ellen. She

happens to be a very respectable and well-brought-up lady. That's the only kind I associate with."

Sue Ellen was taken aback. Never before had he had the nerve to admit to her face that he was cheating on her. She had long known about it, of course, but somehow it was as if she were finding out for the first time. Her anger was fresh and raw.

"Amazing," she gasped, "you don't even have the good manners to lie about it!"

"There wouldn't be any use in lying at this point, would there?" he remarked, smiling a little half-smile.

"I've had it, J.R.," she said, looking right through him. "I won't be humiliated like that ever again! You're gonna change your ways as of right now, or else!"

"Or else what, Sue Ellen?" he taunted her. "There's nothing you can do to stop me, and you know it. Besides, I'm really a nice guy deep down inside. Look at the way I've agreed to accept your little bastard into the family and not make a fuss about it, though the father is probably some drug-addicted mental patient you picked up off a park bench."

Sue Ellen ignored this heavy-handed barb, too overdone to find its mark, and continued laying out her ultimatum as if he hadn't said a word.

"You're going to be a faithful husband and a loving father, just like I build you up to be, and your lifestyle is going to stay that way forever. Because this child *could* be your child, and you can't afford to let it get away from you. Your fooling around is over, do you hear me, J.R.? *Over!*"

"I see," said J.R. quietly, staring right back into her eyes. "And what if I say no?"

"Then you've got yourself a divorce, mister," she replied.

For the first time in their discussion, J.R. broke into a big broad smile, his eyes twinkling wickedly.

"Oh, Sue Ellen, you are funny," he said. "A funny, funny woman. You're not going to give up your money, your position, your prestige, your home, and your future, just because you don't like my lifestyle! Now, I like my life—and my women. I like them a lot, and there's no way I'm going to give them up just because you object. So you'd better just change your mind, 'cause I'm not gonna change my habits."

They looked hard at each other, locked into each other's gazes for more than a full minute, each waiting for the other to flinch. Finally, Sue Ellen saw that she had no choice, that if she were going to win with J.R., she would have to take drastic measures, measures that would risk everything.

"You can take your habits and go to hell with them!" she seethed, and without waiting for him to reply, she swept out of the room, slamming the door loudly behind her.

J.R. wondered if the door's slamming had awoken any of the family. After a few seconds, he was satisfied that no one had heard it. He walked over and poured himself a drink from Sue Ellen's vodka bottle.

She'll come around, he said to himself. Soon enough, she'd see that her life was nothing without him. Then she'd come around.

Cliff Barnes was in his pajamas and just about to turn in when he heard the knocking on the door. Puzzled, he went to answer it.

It was Sue Ellen, still dressed in the clothes she'd worn to Fort Worth, the elegant and flashy scarf draped around her neck, though looking a bit wilted now. She had flown to Cliff's apartment, not even thinking where she was going until she got there. But where else could she have gone? Her mother's? J.R. would find her there in no time and drag her back. A hotel? He'd find her there, too. This was the only place she could hide and think things out. She did not know if she was willing to leave J.R., but she certainly was not going back to him tonight, not if her life depended on it.

Cliff, for his part, was more than a little surprised to see her. He knew instinctively that for her to appear at his door at this hour of the night, with no prior warning, meant that something important had happened. And he had a pretty good idea what it was from the look on her face.

Half-dreading the pain of seeing her again, half-anticipating the pleasure of holding her, he let her in, closing the door behind them.

He fixed her a drink, and she made herself

comfortable, as comfortable as she could feel at such a critical turning point in her life. For the first time, she had actually walked out on J.R., and she didn't know where her decision would lead her. She was afraid and excited, and wanted desperately for Cliff to hold her and comfort her.

She told him about the fight between her and J.R., sobbing a little as she did so, sipping on the drink to warm her blood. She told him she wasn't going back to Southfork, not that night, anyway. In the backs of both their minds was the question of whether there were any circumstances under which she and Cliff might make a go of it together. It was more than a long shot, it was one in a million, but both of them, deep inside, wanted it desperately. But did either have the courage? Knowing it might destroy both of them, would either one take the chance?

"What does it all mean, Sue Ellen?" Cliff wanted to know. "To us." Cliff put his head in his hands. Part of him felt used, knowing as he did that the visit meant, in all probability, more hurt and pain for him, more opening up of old wounds. He wanted her terribly and wished with all his heart that he didn't. She sat there, trembling, her need for him a powerful attractant, and he tried to contain himself, to stop himself from taking her in his arms.

"Sue Ellen," he said, pacing the floor nervously, "you're carrying a child that's probably mine. How do you think that affects me, seeing you like this? I've had to give you up! Did you think I wanted it that way? Do you think I want my child brought up at Southfork? How do you think I'll feel when I see that child walking hand in hand with you down the street, knowing I can never be a part of it? It's killing me that you're here, don't you see that?"

"This is not just a romantic game we're playing, Cliff," she replied, sure of herself and what she was saying. "We've been as close as two people can get. And I need you now. Tonight. Tomorrow may be different, but for now I need you. You can't turn me away. Not after what we've been to each other."

He hung his head. She was right, and he knew it.

"I know it makes it harder for you, my being here. And maybe I'll go back to Southfork tomorrow. But maybe I won't."

He looked up at her. Could it really be possible? His heart leaped in his chest as she came to him, removing his pajama tops, running her hands over his chest as his resistance melted away. Breathing hard, she removed her jacket, unwinding the scarf and dropping it on the back of the couch, where it slid to the floor and out of sight.

But Sue Ellen was not aware of it, nor was Cliff. They had moved beyond the point of noticing anything except each other.

J.R. came down to breakfast the next morning as though nothing had happened. Of course, Sue Ellen's car was not in the driveway, and the family did notice her absence from the breakfast table.

"Where has she gone so early in the morning?" Miss Ellie asked him. "It's not like Sue Ellen to be such an early riser."

J.R. had prepared for this moment while he was getting dressed, and he said his lines just the way he had rehearsed them.

"Oh, she had something special on with her mother today . . . and you know, Momma, since she's been pregnant, she's been getting up early almost every day. Digestion's been acting up on her, I believe. You know how these things are. I don't know exactly what she and her mother are up to. Probably shopping, knowing Sue Ellen." He chuckled fondly, successfully masking any problems.

Miss Ellie put down her napkin. "I really should invite the Shepards out to the ranch," she said remorsefully. "I've just been putting it off and putting it off, but I don't want Sue Ellen's mother to think I'm avoiding her."

"Well," J.R. said, "I think you might have to wait a few days. Sue Ellen mentioned something about how she might spend a few days over at her mother's . . . getting reacquainted, you know, that sort of thing."

He was covering in advance, hedging his bets. He had expected her to return by breakfast, but obviously she was a little madder than usual.

Jock had something else on his mind. "Say, isn't her sister eighteen by now? Same age as you, Lucy." Jock was not fond of the kind of people Lucy liked to hang around with, and thought that Kristin might be a nice new friend for her. "Her bein' new to the neighborhood and all, maybe you could show her around, honey," he suggested.

Lucy rolled her eyes. That was all she needed —a clone of Sue Ellen to hang around with all day. One Sue Ellen was boring and frustrating enough.

"Gee, Grandpa, I don't know. I've got so much schoolwork to do. . . ."

She looked around the table for rescue.

"Don't worry, Lucy," J.R. said, "Kristin's going to be a busy girl around this town. Her momma's got big plans for her, from what I understand."

Bobby and Pam came down to join the others, both in a hurry, and only able to stop for a quick cup of coffee.

Bobby, however, was not dressed in his usual suit. This morning he was wearing jeans. As he told Jock, he was on his way to a meeting with Ray Krebbs.

J.R. perked up his ears. Ray had been a big thorn in his side lately over that Section 40 business, and J.R. was afraid of Bobby getting wind of anything.

"What on earth have you and that cowboy got to discuss?" he asked derisively.

"Oh, he wants to build a house on that land Daddy gave him, and I thought I might be able to give him some advice, that's all."

J.R. snorted in disgust. "That's just dandy. Before you know it, there'll be sharecroppers all over Southfork!"

He stopped, realizing that he had let himself get out of control. Bobby's meeting with Ray was probably completely innocent, and he was succeeding in making a spectacle of himself.

Lucy asked him what he had against Ray, but he wasn't going to get into it. He had had enough. It was time to go look for that damn wife of his and drag her home by her hair if he had to.

He excused himself hurriedly and stalked off to get his car.

Mrs. Shepard's rented house was on a nice, pleasant, respectable street in a middle-class section of the city. The lawns were well cared for, and the cars were no more than four years old. It was not the kind of place where millionaires lived, but it was the kind of place Kristin did not need to be ashamed of if a millionaire arrived in his limousine or his Mercedes to pick her up or drop her off. In fact, a silver Mercedes could be seen coming down the street, pulling up in front of the house.

J.R. Ewing got out and went up the stairs to ring the bell. He looked around for Sue Ellen's car. He didn't see it out front, but the back of the driveway was not in his view, and she might have pulled her car back there, discreetly out of sight.

She had to be here, after all. Where else would she go? To a hotel? Surely not. Not without packing a suitcase! Not Sue Ellen.

Mrs. Shepard answered the door already at

nine in the morning, dressed to receive visitors. She was a woman who believed in the old saw that you never knew when a gentleman might come to call, and it was always best to be prepared. Mrs. Shepard followed her own advice and made sure that her girls did the same.

She was surprised, but of course delighted to see J.R. Somehow she had had the gnawing feeling that he'd been avoiding her and was gratified to see that she'd been mistaken. Holding the door open wide, she ushered him in with a wide sweep of her arm.

He strode by her as if she did not exist, and walked into the hallway, looking left and right for Sue Ellen as he did so. She was nowhere, nowhere that he could see.

"Well," he remarked casually, trying to disguise his concern, "you certainly have gotten this place looking good quickly! What'd it take you, three days?"

The place did indeed look wonderful, tasteful and intimidatingly elegant. Mrs. Shepard was determined to wipe out the memory of her failed, miserable marriage to Mr. Shepard, that no-good louse. She had kept his name, a woman did that, but she was determined to erase any trace of bad taste or boorishness his presence had left on her psyche.

"Why thank you, J.R.," she cooed.

Now, J.R. was a man she could understand and admire. Why Sue Ellen always complained about him she could never understand. After all, a man was entitled to his little lapses every now and then, and if he provided well for his wife, she could be a little more forgiving.

"It's only a rental . . . we haven't made up our minds yet whether we're staying in town for good or not."

By this time J.R. had satisfied himself that Sue Ellen was not in the house and had not come to her mother's at all since leaving Southfork the night before. He needed to find her but hadn't the faintest idea of where to begin looking. He thought his best chance was to go with his original instincts. Sooner or later, if she didn't go back home, she would show up at her mother's. J.R. decided to stay put and let Sue Ellen come to him.

"I guess I beat the little woman here, huh?" he said, trying to sound cheerful.

"Oh . . . I didn't know she was coming!" said Mrs. Shepard, clapping her hands together. Things were definitely looking up.

"Oh, yeah . . ."

He was finding it very hard to be nice to Sue Ellen's mother, a woman who had always made his skin crawl. In J.R.'s opinion, it was Sue Ellen's mother who was responsible for all the qualities in his wife that he didn't like.

"Yeah," he lied, smiling as broadly as his lips would allow him, tight with tension as they were, "we wanted to have a nice visit with you all."

Mrs. Shepard could not believe her ears. "Do sit down, J.R., while I get you some nice coffee and cake!"

"Oh, no, Mrs. Shepard, don't bother, really . . ."

"Patricia," she insisted with an iron smile. "It's Patricia, J.R., and you simply *must* have some coffee."

J.R. smiled and shrugged. He felt as if he'd been gripped in the jaws of some powerful, merciless predator. This was going to be an agonizing wait. Sue Ellen was going to pay for his present discomfort once he got her home again.

"Kristin!" Mrs. Shepard shouted up the stairs as she left the room. "Your brother-in-law is here! Come down and be sociable!"

J.R. was beginning to doubt his original decision to stick around. The last time he'd seen his niece, Kristin, she had been the most awful pre-teen brat imaginable.

He began looking around for some excuse to get out of there, when he looked toward the stairway and froze. Down the stairs came a pair of long, bare, staggeringly sexy legs, followed by a gorgeous set of hips clad only in extremely skimpy running shorts, a midriff that could stop traffic, and at last, the face of an angel with wickedness on its mind—It was Kristin. Sister-in-law or not, J.R. could not help swallowing hard.

"Well, hello, J.R.," she said, coming forward to greet him.

Her voice and manner exuded sensuality. What in the world had happened to Kristin in seven years?

She saw that he was speechless, and decided to help him out.

"I've matured quite a bit since last we met, right?"

J.R. cleared his throat. "You said a mouthful," he agreed.

"Do I remind you of Sue Ellen?" she asked.

There was a resemblance, but if you put the two of them next to each other, there was no contest. Kristin looked like an even more devastating version of what Sue Ellen had looked like at nineteen.

"Most folks say we don't look anything alike."

"Oh, I don't know . . . I think you have some very good points in common."

Kristin sidled up close to him, her eyes never leaving his for an instant.

"Is she coming?" she asked in a hoarse whisper.

"Is who coming?" asked J.R., barely able to concentrate.

"Sue Ellen," she helped him again. "Or is this just you visiting?"

"Oh . . . uh, she ought to be here soon. . . . I think . . ."

Kristin gave him yet another languorous smile.

"Have a seat," she said, patting the empty spot on the sofa next to her. "Let's talk till she arrives."

It was a good thing that Mrs. Shepard reappeared at that moment with the coffee service; J.R. was close to losing his cool completely.

Patricia Shepard's presence was like a bucket of cold water in his face. He quickly recovered himself and his sense of propriety.

"Well," said Mrs. Shepard purposefully, "how do you think our little Kristin turned out?"

J.R. took a deep breath. "You've outdone yourself, Mrs. Shepard, you truly have. Kristin is one very beautiful young lady."

"Call me Patricia," she repeated, putting her hand on his.

He smiled, nauseated, and pulled his hand gently away.

"Patricia," he stated.

"I live for the day when Kristin will find a man like you. I want her to do every bit as well for herself as Sue Ellen has."

Mrs. Shepard was making her pitch, asking J.R. to help find her daughter a husband. J.R. looked Kristin up and down once again, still knocked off balance by the unexpected revelation his little sister-in-law had turned out to be.

"Oh, don't you worry about Kristin, Patricia," he said, smiling right into Kristin's eyes. "She won't have any problems finding herself the perfect man."

"No problems at all," Kristin said, smiling right back into J.R.'s eyes. "What I want, I get."

Chapter Eight

J.R. waited almost an hour with Patricia Shepard and her youngest daughter before finally giving up, making some excuse for his wife and hurrying away. He was now furious with her. She was wasting his time, forcing him into embarrassing situations, and altogether upsetting his balance.

He strode into the office in a black mood, not knowing what to do next. Louella was waiting for him with his messages. There were over a dozen of them, but he leafed through them quickly, tossing them back on the desk until he found the one he was looking for. Sue Ellen had called—from Southfork.

"Did she say anything to you, Louella?"

The secretary nodded. Mrs. Ewing had wanted to know J.R.'s schedule for the morning. Louella had told her J.R. was busy all day.

Taking the messages with him, her boss disappeared into his office. He immediately went over to the phone and called home. Raoul answered, and J.R. waited while he paged Sue Ellen.

"Yes, J.R., what is it?" she said in an impatient tone as she got on the line.

J.R. was a bit taken aback. After all, she was back home . . . she had called him . . . obviously she was repentant and wanted to apologize. So why that haughty tone? He didn't understand.

When he had called home he had been ready to lay down the law to her, but now that she had responded in such an unexpected way, he didn't know how to proceed. What he could not see over the phone was that Sue Ellen was standing in front of two stuffed suitcases, which she had just finished packing.

"I called your office this morning, J.R.," she explained, "to make sure you weren't coming home early today. I didn't want you bursting in on me while I was here."

Suddenly J.R. panicked. As long as he had felt sure that in the end she would cave in, as long as he'd been sure she needed him, he felt sure he'd have his way with her. But now, now that she was talking like this, and he could tell that she meant it, he had to reconsider fast.

"Look, Sue Ellen," he said, trying not to sound too pleading or conciliatory, "let's not be too hasty about all this. I will admit that I got a little bit carried away last night, said some things I shouldn't have. Why don't we get together someplace private where we can talk about things, all right? How 'bout the Cattleman's

Club at four-thirty? I can reserve us a private booth, and—"

She didn't let him get any further. "Look, J.R.," she said, "there's no point in getting together. You and I have nothing to talk about. It's not enough for you to apologize for what you said last night, or even for what you've done the past seven years. I'm not having any apologies anymore. I didn't come back to Southfork to see you, I came back here to pack some things. I'm leaving momentarily, and I don't know when —or if—I'm coming back."

J.R. felt the blood pounding in his temples. What would he do if she actually left? How would he explain it to the family? To his cronies? He could not allow this to happen! It would be too humiliating.

"Where do you think you're going to go, Sue Ellen?" he prodded her, trying both to dissuade her and to get some information out of her. But Sue Ellen had known him for too long and wasn't going to be an easy mark for him any longer.

"It's none of your business where I'm going, J.R.," she said stonily.

"And while we're at it," he continued, beginning to lose his temper and his control, "where were you last night? Huh?"

Sue Ellen smiled. She felt good. Her tactics had finally succeeded in getting to J.R. She finally had his attention after all this time, and she wasn't about to make it easy for him.

"Aw, poor J.R.," she taunted him. "He's so worried about his little Sue Ellen! If she doesn't come back today, what's he going to tell the family when dinnertime rolls around and his wifey's not there beside him? Is he going to tell them about his floozies? About his lying, cheating ways? Whatever will his daddy and momma say?"

J.R.'s voice was dark with hatred and fury. "I explained your absence this morning, Sue Ellen. You'd better not make me go through that again."

Sue Ellen smiled triumphantly. "That's exactly what I'm going to do, J.R. I'm going to make you do it again and again until you finally have to tell the truth to your family, and yourself. The truth is I'm leaving you, J.R. And deep in that black withered heart of yours you know why." She hung up the phone, slamming it down on the receiver.

J.R. sat there for a moment, thinking about murder. After a moment, he came back to earth and buzzed his secretary. Murder may not have been possible or appropriate, but there were still concrete measures to be taken. Certain precautions . . .

He asked Louella to call a man at City Bank for him, then stared silently out the window for what seemed to him an inordinately long time before the connection was made. Damn bankers . . . kept you waiting just to prove their own importance. Finally, Jack Simpson got on the line. He was the Ewings' "personal banker," who handled the family's day-to-day accounts and cash flow.

"Hi, Jack, J.R. Ewing here," J.R. said, trying

to sound cheerful. "Listen, do me a favor, will you? Sue Ellen went and did a dumb thing . . . left her wallet in the store and got it stolen. Thing is, her checkbook was in it, and all her credit cards. We don't know if they'll turn up or not, but in the meantime, would you put a freeze on her account, and on those cards, too? Better freeze up her savings account too, while you're at it . . . never know . . . good boy . . . I sure do appreciate it. Listen, why don't you bring the wife and kids out to the Ewing rodeo next month. Love to see you. . . . Great . . . Bye-bye, Jack, and thanks again."

He hung up, and sat back in his chair. So, she wanted war, did she? Well, he'd give her war . . . and he'd give it to her J.R. Ewing style. When he got through with her, she'd crawl back to Southfork!

By the time Sue Ellen had managed to assemble all the little items she thought she might need for an extended stay, it was almost four o'clock. She descended the stairs, lugging her two huge suit-cases in either hand, the weight all the harder for her to bear because of her pregnancy.

As she got to the bottom of the stairs, Bobby entered through the front door, his meeting with Ray over. He stopped still when he saw her loaded down with her bags, not quite under-standing what he was looking at.

"I didn't know you were home, Bobby," she said, just to have something to say.

"J.R. said you were going to be at your mother's house," he countered.

She smiled wanly. "I guess we were both mistaken, then," she said, feeling stupid.

She started past him on her way to the door, when he stopped her with a hand on her arm.

"Would you like me to help you carry those?" he offered. He was beginning to put two and two together. "Or maybe you'd like to have a talk —just for a minute or two?"

This was not what Sue Ellen had expected. "I don't know what you mean, Bobby," she muttered.

"Well," he gestured to the suitcases, "it's not every day we meet like this. You're all packed and on your way out the door. Want to tell me what this is all about?"

"I didn't know you cared, Bobby," she said, looking him in the eye for the first time.

"Why? Have I ever given you any reason to believe I didn't care, Sue Ellen?"

He hadn't, actually. But in the seven years that Sue Ellen had lived at Southfork, Bobby had never approached her as a friend, never tried to carry on a one-on-one conversation with her, never opened up to her as he seemed to do so easily with everybody else. She had often resented his easy manner, the way Jock and Ellie seemed to favor him over J.R.

"I never would have thought you cared about me in the least, Bobby, if you want to know the truth," she said flatly. "I always thought we were just two acquaintances who happened to live under the same roof with each other."

Bobby blinked, stung by her words. "If that's

true, Sue Ellen, I think it's because you always shut me out."

She sighed impatiently. It didn't matter in the least anymore since they were never going to become friends now. No use crying over spilled milk, even if it was the milk of human kindness.

"Whatever," she said quickly. "The truth of the matter is I'm leaving your brother. I've had about all I can take."

Bobby moved in front of her. He didn't want to let her leave just like that, without even a word, a touch between acquaintances.

"Listen," he began haltingly, searching for the right words to express his feelings at this very difficult moment. "I know I'm in no position to dispense words of wisdom about my brother and you. But if things are not good between you, it's not the end of the world, is it? I mean, everybody has problems. You've got to work on them . . . talk it out . . . isn't there some other way besides leaving without even saying good-bye?"

Sue Ellen laughed bitterly. "Think about it, Bobby," she whispered. "You've known your brother all your life. You know what he's like, how he is. Well, I've lived with him for seven long years, and I've had enough. I don't have to put up with that kind of abuse. Not now, and not ever again."

She stopped, catching herself. She hadn't meant to let herself get angry, not in front of Bobby. After all, it wasn't his fault she was leaving, and she hadn't meant to share her problems with him, let alone lash out that way.

"Bobby," she said, a plea in her voice for

understanding, for sympathy. "You know how much I love living here, how much my hopes were set on a future here . . . do you really believe I'd just walk out without trying to salvage things? I've tried everything, Bobby. Everything. There's just no other way, believe me."

"But you're pregnant, now, Sue Ellen," he pointed out. "Isn't that a reason to stay and try again?"

She smiled sadly, holding her hand to her womb and sighing. "I always thought this child would bring us closer together . . . all those years I wanted this more than anything . . . but I see now that it hasn't. Things have been worse than ever. Listen, Bobby," she said, gathering herself to get on her way, "I need to get out of here before he decides to come home and stop me. You said you wanted to help me with the bags. Does the offer still hold?"

He smiled and embraced her warmly. "I wish you the best, Sue Ellen, I really do." And with that, he reached for her bags.

She smiled fondly at him. He really was a good person.

"If you want to know more about it all, why don't you ask J.R.?" she suggested. "I'm sure he'll have plenty to say about it," she said as she swept past him out the door.

Cliff Barnes was sitting in his office, thinking deeply. His secretary, Agnes, entered the room quietly, so as not to disturb him, and laid some papers on his desk. She slid the papers in front of him, took his empty coffee cup, and tiptoed out of the room, all without a word.

The click of the closing door woke Cliff out of his reverie, and he came to with a start. There in front of him lay the papers Agnes had brought —a catalogue of Dallas zoning regulations. He had asked her for them the day before. He had wanted to study them, to see just what rules he was being asked to break. He looked blankly at them now.

Last night had been a watershed period in his life, and he felt as if he had now been washed up on the other side of a sea. Sue Ellen's visit had shaken him deeply. Not since his boyhood days had he let himself fall in love with a woman the way he had with Sue Ellen. He had luxuriated in his feelings simply because he had always known that Sue Ellen would never leave J.R., would never give up the privileges of being a Ewing just to run to his side. He could safely give his heart in the knowledge that it would just as safely be broken in the end, and that he would never have to lose his treasured freedom.

But last night had changed all that. He knew now that, in spite of her pregnancy, Sue Ellen would sooner or later ask to move in with him. It had forced him to think about things in a new way, to examine his original feelings for her, his motives in wooing her, and his plans and fears for his future. He remembered what she had said about playing games, how their whole relationship, beautiful as it had been, had really been an elaborate game. But now it had the potential to become a reality. Cliff was frightened and excited by the prospect. But he wasn't sure he had it in him. Not sure at all . . .

J.R. arrived home from work at about five, having left a bit early in hopes of catching Sue Ellen at home and talking some sense into her head. He saw Bobby sitting at one of the patio tables and went over to question him.

"Have you seen Sue Ellen, Bobby?" he asked.

"Sure have, J.R. She left about half an hour ago."

Damn, J.R. thought, and turned to go into the house.

"She had two big suitcases with her," Bobby added, which stopped J.R. in his tracks.

"Oh, did she now?" he said breezily, trying to cover. "I guess her momma persuaded her to spend some serious time over there, getting reacquainted . . ."

"J.R.," Bobby said, feeling it best to be blunt with his ever-devious brother, "she said she was walking out on you."

J.R. stared hard at his brother. What did he have to do with Sue Ellen's leaving? Had he helped talk her into it? No, J.R. decided, Bobby wouldn't stoop that low.

"So," he said with a quick laugh, "she took you into her confidence, did she? After all these years? Just decided to make a friend out of you. You mean to tell me she just walked right up to you and started crying on your shoulder?"

"No, J.R., it wasn't like that. I saw her

leaving and asked her about it . . . I asked if I could do anything to help change her mind."

J.R. was really mad now. He was angry at Sue Ellen, but the fact that Bobby had not physically restrained her until he'd gotten home made him turn his anger toward Bobby instead.

"Listen, little brother, if I ever need your help, I'll ask you for it, all right? What made you think Sue Ellen and I needed your counsel?"

Bobby stood up, annoyed. "She was walking out with two suitcases, J.R. I thought that was reason enough. Oh, and by the way, when I mentioned the baby as a reason to stay, she laughed and said it was just another reason to go. She said I ought to ask you about that. Said you'd explain . . ."

J.R. took a moment to calm down. "Bobby, let's get one thing straight," he said after a moment. "We're brothers, and we'll always be brothers. But you are not my marriage counselor, or my psychiatrist, or even my friend. You handle your own marriage, and I'll take care of mine."

On that note, he wheeled and strode off into the house. Bobby looked after him, shaken by his brother's anger, and wondering what had provoked such an overreaction.

Meanwhile, J.R., upon entering the house, went straight to the telephone in the den. Things had gone far enough and now it was time to break out the heavy artillery.

"Put Dan Marsh on the phone, please. Tell him it's J.R. Ewing," he whispered.

Soon the voice of J.R.'s trusty private investigator came on the line.

"Dan," he said darkly, "don't talk. Just listen. I want you to put a tail on my wife, Sue Ellen. Find out what she's up to, where she goes, who she sees, everyone she speaks with. Understand? You'll find her, sooner or later, at her mother's —11511 Royal Oak . . . This is a big one, Dan, understand? Put your best men on it . . . Thanks. Talk to you soon . . . bye."

He hung up, satisfied to wait for now, having done all that had to be done. She was not going to get away with this. As sure as his name was J.R. Ewing, she was going to be back at South-fork before the week was out, the obedient wife once again.

141

Chapter Nine

Sue Ellen got in the car and just drove. She had no idea where she was going; she only knew she wanted to get away from Southfork, as far away as she could go. She just let the car take her where it wanted to go, and two hours later she had gotten herself completely lost. She cruised down unfamiliar streets at untoward speeds, the tears streaming down her cheeks, as the sun set and evening became night.

Finally, she noticed that she was running low on gas and turned into a station nearby. She got out of the car and headed for the rest room. She badly needed to fix her makeup. Wherever she was going tonight, she didn't want whoever was there to see her like this.

When she returned to the car, she asked the attendant where she was and was surprised when he told her. She had taken a completely random course and had wound up not five blocks from her mother's house.

Feeling there must have been some method in her madness, and that this was somehow meant to happen this way, she got back into the car. She actually began to feel happy, to feel that she was in some way in harmony with the universe.

Getting out of the car in front of her mother's house, and glad to see by all the lights that someone was at home, she took one bag with her and went up the front walk.

Mrs. Shepard answered the door, freshly powdered as ever, with the same frozen smile on her face as always. When she saw who her visitor was, the smile vanished, replaced by a look of utmost concern. She opened the door wide to admit her daughter. The suitcase in Sue Ellen's hand caught her attention at once, and, being a woman of quick intelligence, she had an excellent idea of what was going on.

She knew enough not to say anything about the suitcase, or even about how strange it was for her daughter to show up on her doorstep unannounced so late in the evening. She knew she had to wait for Sue Ellen to explain and that her daughter certainly would tell her by and by, or she would not have come to her in the first place.

"How nice to see you again, Sue Ellen," she began in her best light-hearted tone. "J.R. was over to see us just this morning, and mentioned that you might be coming by . . ." She trailed off, hoping Sue Ellen would pick up the conversation from there.

"He probably wanted to know if I'd been staying here," Sue Ellen said, searching the older woman's face for the truth. "Right, Mother?"

Mrs. Shepard nodded, still waiting. "I brought my suitcases, Mother, or didn't you notice?"

Why did her mother always have to play it so cool, even with her? It drove Sue Ellen crazy.

"They're very nice bags, Sue Ellen," Mrs. Shepard commented, feeling the expensive soft leather. "Who bought them for you, dear?"

The remark was well aimed, and Sue Ellen felt it hit its mark right in her gut.

"J.R. got them for me, of course, as if you didn't know. It's the perfect luggage for the wife of a successful multimillionaire, don't you think? Of course you do."

Mrs. Shepard held her ground. "Being married to a millionaire has its good points, Sue Ellen. Don't forget that."

"I've lived with J.R. Ewing for seven long years, Mother," cried Sue Ellen, "and his few good points have worn thin."

Mrs. Shepard put her arms around her daughter's shoulders. "You've forgotten, Sue Ellen. You've gotten used to being rich, and powerful, and you need to be reminded of what life is like without all that. J.R. has done an awful lot for you, and you should be a little more appreciative."

Sue Ellen broke away from her mother's serpentine embrace. "Yes," she remembered, "you always did like to remind me. All my youth I remember you drumming it into me . . . how I had to marry a wealthy man . . . that they were the only ones good enough for me. You worked so hard, Mother. And you were successful, too. I'm the perfect wife for a wealthy man, but no one is perfect for J.R."

"You *are* the perfect wife for him, darling," she persisted. "J.R.'s no different than any other man of his position. He has his little foibles, just like they all do. But ever since your father died, I have worked to make you two girls perfect. And you are perfect, my dear. You and J.R. will work this out, you'll see. I'll help you. It'll be all right. Just be patient."

Kristin had appeared on the staircase in time to overhear the tail end of the conversation and was obviously lingering there, not knowing whether to go back upstairs or come down to join them.

"Kristin," said Sue Ellen, "you might as well hear this. Maybe you'll learn something that'll help you avoid the kind of trouble I wound up getting into. I know Momma's pulling the same business on you now that she used to do with me. You ought to see how it all turned out. Maybe you'll change your mind about a few things."

Kristin sidled down the stairs, smirking disdainfully at her sister. "Gee, Sue Ellen," she purred, "I don't know . . . J.R. seems like a really fantastic guy to me. Just the kind of man I'd want."

Sue Ellen gasped in disbelief. Her mother had gone to work on Kristin, and in a big way, too.

This girl was even more a product of her mother's making than she herself had been at nineteen.

Mrs. Shepard smiled contentedly and nodded encouragingly as her younger daughter spoke. She would have agreed with Sue Ellen that she had done a job on her younger daughter, but their opinions of the result would have differed.

Sue Ellen paced the room a bit, studying the two of them. She had to speak her mind to them, had to try to reach Kristin before it was too late. Her mother was far beyond hope, but Kristin was still young. Young enough to save from disaster . . . or at least try to save.

"You taught me many things, Momma," she began. "But there were a few items you left out."

"Which you are now obviously about to tell us," Mrs. Shepard concluded.

"Yes. Tell me this, Mother—what do you do when every night you're alone in your bed? When your husband never touches you? When he saves all his loving for whoever happens to be his latest floozy? How do I live with knowing that at the very moment I'm most alone, he's with somebody else? Somebody he doesn't even care about!"

She didn't cry. She couldn't cry. Suddenly all her tears had dried up.

Mrs. Shepard and Kristin were equally clear-eyed. Neither one of them seemed to have the slightest sympathy for her situation.

"A lot of men cheat on their wives, Sue Ellen," her mother reminded her. "And a lot of wives put up with it. There are far worse things to have to put up with in a marriage. Like poverty, and insecurity, and shame . . ."

"I can't believe," Kristin said, shaking her head in disbelief, "that you would risk everything you have just to have J.R. all to yourself! He must be some kind of guy for you to get all that hot about his cheating on you!"

Kristin had found J.R. attractive from the moment she had met him. She had only been eleven years old, but even then she had been crazy about him. At that time, he had ignored her little childlike advances completely. But that past morning, when they had met again, she was sure he had noticed her, and that he had been extremely pleased with what he'd seen. If Sue Ellen was going to be so stupid as to leave J.R. over nothing, well, she herself might even consider stepping into the gap. . . .

Sue Ellen did not guess what was going on in her sister's mind. She only saw that having a husband who cheated on her would not bother Kristin. She found it hard to believe that any woman would put up with it. But she failed to understand the difference between herself and her little sister.

Sue Ellen had always been a sensitive child, much as her father was. Kristin was more like their mother. It was money, power and prestige alone that aroused Kristin. When Sue Ellen had met J.R., his riches had attracted her, certainly, but she had also been in love with him, or she would not have married. Kristin would have no such prerequisites. Love and money were inseparable to her.

"And what about the baby you're carrying, Sue Ellen?" her mother pointed out. "J.R. gave you a baby, too! On top of everything else! You should be on your knees with gratitude!"

Sue Ellen bit her tongue and found herself saying, "That's very amusing, Mother. Very amusing."

"Well, I don't see anything funny about it," snapped her mother, who was seriously annoyed at the thickness her elder daughter was displaying. "Do you know what it means to leave your husband? Do you realize that I stayed with your father until the day he died? Just think about that! I stayed with him, though he had so little to offer in comparison with a man like J.R.! You *can't* leave J.R.! You just *can't!* I won't allow it!"

Sue Ellen looked to Kristin. "You understand, Kristin? Do you understand me at all?"

But the girl's face was hard, unsympathetic. "Sure I understand you, Sue Ellen. You decided having J.R. wasn't enough for you. You had to have him exclusively. And you were crazy enough to leave him entirely and give up everything you have in life, just to get him all to yourself. I understand you all right. But don't expect me to feel sorry for you. You made your own bed; you can lie in it."

Sue Ellen sighed deeply. It was useless. She had tried her best, and hadn't even made a dent. They were both blind as bats. Blinded by wealth. She wished she could arrange for them to have it for a while. Then they'd understand. Or would they? Sue Ellen had the sickening feeling that deep down inside these two women were hearts made of pure cold steel.

"Speaking of beds," she said, changing the subject, "can I stay here tonight? It's why I came, not to argue. Of course, I could go to a hotel . . . probably should have . . ."

"Nonsense, dear!" cried her mother, forgetting the quarrel instantly, realizing that with her daughter still under her roof, it was still in her power to save the marriage her daughter seemed so intent on ruining. A call to J.R., a few choice words in Sue Ellen's ears, and perhaps all this would be just a bad memory. "Don't you dare go to a hotel! What's family for? We may disagree from time to time, but you're still my daughter, and I'm still your mother."

Suddenly Sue Ellen felt like crying. Awful as her mother was, she was the only mother Sue Ellen had. The sadness of that fact overwhelmed her, and her eyes brimmed over with tears of gratitude. Mrs. Shepard led her tenderly up the stairs, all sweetness and love now.

It was still seven months away. The day when J.R.'s first child would be born. But the family had been waiting for many years, and as soon as the happy news of Sue Ellen's pregnancy had been announced, Miss Ellie had gone right to work, making the house ready to receive its future owner. She had fussed over the furniture, the layette, the nursery and even the playroom. In the beginning Sue Ellen had helped her, and the two of them had had some wonderful times together, shopping and planning and getting each other excited.

Now, suddenly, Sue Ellen had disappeared. Miss Ellie, wise woman that she was, could tell that something had happened between Sue Ellen and J.R., something dramatic and critical, and that their marriage was in mortal danger. She felt bad about that, partly for her son, and partly because she had grown fond of Sue Ellen over the years and would miss her if she weren't around. But mostly she grieved that the baby, her second grandchild, would not grow up at Southfork with her, with its family, where it belonged. All her plans seemed about to go up in smoke, and she stood in the nursery, the morning sun shining in, and felt herself fighting back tears.

The nursery was finished, decorated in a bright canary yellow. Ellie wondered if the baby would ever sleep in its little crib. She knew that if Sue Ellen and J.R. got divorced, things would not be pretty, or friendly, between them. She was worried sick, her head light and her stomach in knots, but she tried to carry on as best she could.

Suddenly Lucy burst into the room, an old bassinet in her arms.

"Yech," Lucy said, wiping the dust off herself. "You'd think Sue Ellen didn't have enough money to buy a new one!"

"That happens to have been *your* bassinet, my dear young lady, so don't you go talking about it like that." Lucy had been the first Ewing grand-

child, and that had been eighteen long years ago.
"I just wanted to see a baby lying in that old
bassinet again. . . ." Ellie lamented.

"Gee, Grandma, I would have thought you
would throw this thing out after what happened
when I was born . . . not what I'd call 'the lucky
bassinet,' is it?"

Lucy had never been one to value tact and
gentility very highly. Her brashness was a product of her hard upbringing; her parents had left
her to be raised by rich grandparents who pampered her. In reminding Miss Ellie of her father's
running away, and her mother's being driven
away by J.R., leaving Lucy behind, she had
pushed Miss Ellie very close to tears. Even Lucy
could see the effect of her hastily spoken words
and tried to soften the blow.

"Gee, Grandma, I didn't mean it that way
. . . stupid me . . . I never think before I talk,
do I? Don't worry—lightning never strikes twice
in the same bassinet, right? Little J.R. the third
should live a charmed life, if you believe in the
law of averages!"

Her forced cheerfulness did nothing to mitigate her insensitivity, but her assumption that
the baby was going to be a boy caught Miss Ellie
by surprise and distracted her attention from her
own sorrow.

"How can you be so sure it won't be a girl?"
she asked.

"Well, if it is, J.R.'ll probably send it back to
the manufacturer, so it'd better be a boy!"

Ellie burst out laughing. It was true, all right.

J.R. was intent on being the father of the next Ewing giant. Ellie, too, felt sure it would be a boy.

She kissed her granddaughter on the cheek before Lucy took off downstairs. When she had gone, Ellie looked around again, and suddenly her depression returned. She could not help the little sobs.

Coming down the hallway, Jock heard them. He stood silently in the doorway, observing his wife, knowing exactly what she was going through. He had to do something. Without alerting her to his presence, he continued down the stairs at an urgent clip and left the house.

Jock was still going full tilt when he arrived at the Ewing building. If he could have pushed the elevator to the top floor to make it go faster, he would have. When the doors finally opened, he burst out like a bull out of a holding pen. Striding right past the amazed receptionist and secretaries, he threw open the door of J.R.'s office and stormed inside.

"You wanna tell me what the hell this is all about?" he said, pounding his hand on J.R.'s desk.

J.R. was taken completely aback by his father's sudden appearance. But J.R. Ewing was a cool customer, and he instantly gathered himself together.

"What what is about, sir?"

"What all this between you and Sue Ellen is about, that's what!" the old man shouted. "You know as well as I do that she left yesterday and took two big suitcases with her. Teresa told me she looked mighty upset, too."

J.R. cleared his throat. He did not smile, did not try to fool his father by making light of the situation. Jock Ewing would not be appeased so easily. Not at this point, anyway.

"Well, Daddy, Sue Ellen and I have been having a few little problems lately . . . nothing to worry about, though. We'll straighten them out in a few days, I'm sure."

Jock paced the room, unsatisfied with his son's response. The image of his saddened wife was fresh in his mind, and in the back of his consciousness was his own fear and rage at the prospect of losing his grandchild.

"J.R., you and Sue Ellen been married seven years now. You had seven years to have problems. Don't tell me you waited till she got pregnant to have a crisis! She's gonna have a baby, man, don't you realize that? You can't let her get away now! Not now!"

"Sir, I don't know how to explain it, but ever since Sue Ellen found out she was pregnant, she's been acting mighty peculiar. Maybe it's hormones or something, I don't know. But there's just been no reasoning with her lately. It wasn't my choice for us to have problems right now."

Jock Ewing wasn't about to tolerate his son's blaming his problems on somebody else. A man had to take total responsibility for things working out right, or he never would. Jock knew that, and he knew that J.R. knew it, too.

"J.R.," he said, ignoring the blame cast upon Sue Ellen, "your mother's down in the dumps. If you could have seen her this morning, your heart would have shriveled up and died. She's got all her hopes pinned on having that grandchild at Southfork. And dammit, so have I."

J.R. bowed his head and nodded. He knew how much the baby meant to his father and mother. He wanted it as much for their sakes as for his own—more even. His whole life was devoted to making his father proud of him, and he wanted more than anything to present him with this baby. But Sue Ellen was ruining everything.

"Now I don't want to hear any more of this bushwa," Jock said, pointing his finger at his son. "Your mother and I want Sue Ellen back at the ranch, and we're counting on you to bring her home. Don't let us down, J.R. Whatever you have to do, do it. But bring Sue Ellen home."

"Yes, sir," J.R. said again. "I will, sir."

Jock nodded, satisfied. "Now, I'm going back home and tell your momma that you're gonna bring Sue Ellen back home. Don't make a liar out of me, you hear?" And he walked out, not even waiting for a reply.

J.R. stared at the door. The stakes had been plainly laid out in front of him. If he had had reason to pursue this matter before, he had more of a reason now. His father's approval was depending on it. "Whatever I have to do, sir," he muttered, "consider it done."

* * *

When Sue Ellen awoke in the morning, she felt worse than ever. She knew she could not stay where she was. Last night she had felt as if the world outside had ceased to exist, that tomorrow would never come. She had finally gotten some badly needed sleep. But when the morning came, she knew she had to get out, that she could not spend even one more night under her mother's roof.

Mrs. Shepard would certainly call J.R. and begin to manipulate a reconciliation. Sue Ellen knew the power of her mother's personality, and in her vulnerable state, she knew she had to leave right away. Not knowing who else to call, she went into the living room at an opportune moment when her mother was in the back, making breakfast, and Kristin was still asleep. She quickly dialed Cliff Barnes' number.

He could tell right away that she was terribly upset. She said she had to see him right away. She knew how upset it made him when she called like this, but she couldn't help herself; she was in trouble and needed to see him.

He could not refuse her. He had never been able to say no to her, and now was certainly not the time for him to begin. They arranged to meet at his apartment at noon.

When the time came for her to leave, she snuck out and was away from the house before her mother noticed she was gone. But as her car pulled away from the curb, so did another one. And it parked just a half block behind her when she got out at Cliff Barnes' house.

When Cliff answered the door, Sue Ellen breezed past him into the room. Her back to him, she said, "Let me speak my piece, Cliff. Please, don't say a word until I'm finished. Okay?"

"Whatever you say, Sue Ellen," he agreed. He did not approach her, sensing her need for distance.

"A lot has happened since yesterday, Cliff. I've thought things through a lot. I considered what all the things in my life mean to me. What it means to be married to J.R. What it means that I'm in love with you. What it means to be carrying this baby, not knowing whose it is, but thinking it's probably yours. And I've decided that, in spite of everything I have, I can't go on like this. I can't go on sleeping alone, unloved, with a baby who'll be brought up to be just like J.R. I'm going to leave him, Cliff. I don't want to be the kind of woman who cheats on her husband just to get a little love. I'm leaving him."

There was a long silence.

"I'm finished now," she said, in case he thought there was more.

But that was not why Cliff remained silent. He did not say anything because he did not know what to say.

"Well, come on, how about a little reaction? Don't you have anything to say? How do you feel about it?"

Cliff blinked. "If it wasn't for us, would you still be leaving him?" he wanted to know.

"Probably," she said, "but this was a major reason."

Cliff shifted uncomfortably. "And what did you think you would do once you left him?"

Sue Ellen felt stung. Was he telling her he didn't want her? After she had run to him, sacrificing everything? Is that why he was acting so distant?

"You don't want me, is that it?" she said, voicing her thoughts. "I thought we might be able to make a life together. You did say you loved me . . . and there's the baby . . . I thought you'd want it."

"But what about J.R.?" he insisted. "You don't seriously believe he's going to take this lying down! Not once he finds out who it is you're with!"

"Are you so afraid of J.R. that you'd give in to him without a fight?" she said, challenging him. "That's the way his daddy walked all over your daddy, isn't it? J.R. would never have been born if Jock hadn't stolen Miss Ellie from Digger . . . that's what you always told me. And now you're going to step aside and let J.R. take away the woman you love, and your child? Do you *really* love me, Cliff? Or were you just using me to get back at J.R.?"

Her arrows had found their mark. And he really did love Sue Ellen, as much as he had ever loved anyone. Nevertheless, he had to be sure of one thing.

"How do I know," he asked, "that *you're* not just using *me* as a way to get back at J.R.? Do you really love me that much?"

"Cliff," she said in a whisper, "you're the only man I ever loved who loved me back, who saw me as a person, not as a slave. Of course I love you."

"All right, Sue Ellen," he said, satisfied. "We'll try. It's all we can do. J.R.'ll make it hard for us. You'll be a lot poorer than you're used to. I'm no J.R. Ewing. I'm not even upper middle-class! But I do want you. And the baby. We'll try."

They reached out to each other, grimly knowing that life would be difficult. But try as they might, neither one of them could begin to realize how difficult their lives were about to become. Or how soon the axe was about to fall.

Later in the day, about two-thirty, Cliff finally managed to get himself out of bed and get dressed. Sue Ellen lingered, at peace for the moment, happy deep down inside. She was where she wanted to be and was genuinely excited about her future with Cliff. Although she knew she would miss being a Ewing, she did not think she would miss it all that much.

As Cliff was tying his tie, the doorbell rang. They looked at each other. Who could it be? Had J.R. found them already? Cliff put his finger to his lips, signifying quiet, and went to answer the door.

Pam was the last person he had expected to see at this hour of the day, and he could not imagine why she had come. Then he saw his custom-made suit in her hand. Of course. She had said she would bring it by.

"I'm impressed," he joked. "You got it for me in thirty-six hours! That's pull!" And he took the suit from her, gesturing for her to come in.

Pam looked around Cliff's living room. It was a mess. Cocktail glasses were everywhere, the cushions of the couch were all askew, and the air smelled distinctly of one-hundred-dollar-an-ounce perfume. Pam, too, was impressed. Her brother had always been a womanizer, but his tastes in women seemed to be getting more expensive, just like his taste in suits.

"Maybe I ought to come back another time?" she said, wondering if she had interrupted something.

"No, no," Cliff assured her. "The usual mess is all you're interrupting. Bachelor apartment, you know."

"Who's the new lady this time, Cliff? Somebody with money, obviously . . . cultivating your political connections, are you?"

"What are you," he complained good-humoredly, "my sister or my governess? Listen, I'm late for a meeting, and I'm not giving interviews right now."

Pam laughed. She loved Cliff's sense of humor. It was his saving grace when all else failed him.

"Don't pay any attention to me," she said. "I'm just going to do a little cleaning up around here. I can't stand it that you live like this."

"So!" he cried gleefully, "you are my governess after all!" And he went into the bedroom to finish dressing.

Pam picked up all the glasses first and deposited them in the sink, then went to straighten the couch. That was when the scarf caught her eye. It was a very distinctive scarf, the kind you buy at one-of-a-kind boutiques. And this scarf was one she had seen before.

Now that she thought of it, the perfume was equally familiar. She was holding the scarf up and staring at it when Cliff came back in.

"What's going on between you and Sue Ellen?" she asked directly.

Cliff saw that it was useless to bluff his sister, so he went to her and grabbed the scarf, stuffing it into his pocket.

"Mind your own beeswax," he muttered.

"I think this is my business, Cliff," she replied. "Sue Ellen is a member of my family now. I'm shocked, frankly. I don't call myself one of J.R.'s greatest fans, but I never thought you would stoop so low just to get back at him!"

"No! That's not it at all! She came to me! She wanted help adopting a baby, for God's sake! I didn't plan it this way!"

"Come on, now, Cliff—it takes two to tango. Besides, there are plenty of lawyers in the world. Don't tell me she just found your name in the Yellow Pages! Cliff, don't you realize you're playing with fire? You fooled around with J.R.'s secretary once, and that was bad enough. But this! This is his wife! Don't you know he'll destroy you when he finds out? And who could blame him? By the way, did you know she was pregnant? Or didn't she tell you that?"

Cliff had to turn away from her to avoid telling her the truth about the baby. Finally he gathered himself enough to admit that he knew she was pregnant.

"Now go, Pam, please," he said softly. "Leave me alone."

How he wished he could tell her the truth. But he couldn't. Not yet. She walked out the door, still incredulous. He could only hope she would hold her tongue out of loyalty to him.

Sue Ellen emerged from the bedroom, a worried look on her face. They held each other, the fear beginning to take hold.

Dan Marsh called his employer to say that they had something for him, but he refused to discuss it on the phone. That was an ominous sign. Marsh had never done that before.

So when the detective arrived at his office, J.R. dismissed his secretaries for the day, and, ushering Marsh in, offered him a drink first. Marsh declined. Another ominous sign.

"Well, Dan," J.R. began, "let me have it. What's the bad news? It must be mighty bad for you to come all this way to tell me."

"Yes sir, it is," Marsh said softly. "We did as you asked. No problem tailing your wife. She never caught on to it, and her movements were easy to follow. She's been at a man's apartment twice in the last twenty-four hours. Since we knew who he was, we checked back a ways and discovered that they've been seeing each other for about two months now. Almost always at his place."

J.R. blinked back tears. Of rage? Of shame? He did not know. "Hit me with the name, Dan. I can take it," he said, biting his lip.

Instead of saying anything, Marsh handed him the folder containing the report. J.R. opened it slowly and stared down at the last name in the world he ever expected to see —CLIFF BARNES.

He stood stock still for a long moment, trying to recover from the shock and not show anything that might be construed as weakness, even to himself.

"Well, well," he finally managed to mumble. "Cliff Barnes. I give Sue Ellen credit. I never would have thought of him . . ." He fell silent again, and Marsh asked him if they should keep tailing her.

"Oh, yes, by all means. Tail her till I tell you not to," J.R. said emphatically. "I've put this off for a long time, but I can't put it off any longer. I'm gonna have to take care of Cliff Barnes so that he never bothers me again."

Chapter Ten

Pam was shaken; there was no question about it. Rushing into the den, she went straight over to the bar and poured herself a drink. Now, for Pam to drink at all was not the usual thing. Downing a stiff one in a single gulp was definitely not her style.

So when Bobby happened to come into the room, and saw what his wife was up to, he knew something had upset her terribly. Since she had come from work, he assumed it was a problem with the job.

"Bad day at the office, huh," he said, tongue-in-cheek.

"Worse than that," she said, leaning against the bar.

"It's okay with me if you give notice," he offered, still teasing her a bit.

"It's got nothing to do with that," she said, shaking her head. "It's . . . it's everything

163

. . . life . . . it's all confused." She wondered how she could share her feelings with him without letting the cat out of the bag. "The Ewings are supposed to wear the black hats, and the Barnes the white ones . . . but everybody wears shades of gray, don't they? You just can't pigeon-hole people, can you? They're much too complicated. Oh, Bobby, I'm so confused."

"Why don't you just tell me what's upsetting you, honey," he suggested. "Maybe I can help?" He stroked her hair tenderly. "Is it really something so terrible?"

She held her breath for a moment, wondering what she should say.

"I don't know, Bobby. That's just it . . . I can't trust my own judgments of people anymore. It used to be I looked at J.R. and I saw only a big bad heartless millionaire. I looked at Cliff, and I saw a white knight. But there really isn't all that much difference between the two of them, is there? Barnes, Ewing, it all comes down to the same thing, doesn't it?"

Bobby was trying hard to grasp his wife's meaning. Obviously there was something she was reluctant to tell him, and just as obviously she was talking about J.R. and Cliff.

"I hope you're not lumping your husband into that same gray category," he said. "You *know* I'm a white knight—not a bad bone in my body—got the X-rays to prove it."

Pam tried to laugh, but it was hard for her. She had never in her wildest dreams imagined a situation was possible where she would side with J.R. against her brother. But the sanctity of marriage was very important to her, and she could not help feeling the way she did. She was learning a very difficult lesson—how to see people as people, and not just in terms of the roles they play. At the moment, it was all too much for her to take in. In time she would adjust, learn to look at the world in a more complicated, thoughtful way.

"Bobby," she said, moving away from him toward the door, "what say we go out for the evening . . . go to town, have a nice elegant dinner, maybe take in a show. In fact—why don't we stay over in town tonight, get a suite in a hotel, make a night of it." She sidled close to him, stroking his cheek. "I don't want to mingle with the family tonight. Let's be just the two of us, alone. I need things to be simple for a few hours, okay?"

Bobby did not need to be convinced any further. He was always willing to spend time with his wife. Being around her made his heart swell with love. If she couldn't tell him what was bothering her, she must have a very good reason for not doing so. And maybe, later, when they were alone together, maybe then she'd let him know her secret.

Nodding, he put his arm around her and gently led her from the room.

Cliff arrived at his office feeling good, feeling strong, feeling that he was doing the right thing. In spite of whatever J.R. might do, he and Sue Ellen would somehow get through it together.

After all, they loved each other, didn't they? And she was carrying his baby, he was sure of it. Things were going to be all right.

And so, he was more than a little taken aback when he opened his office door to find the model Maxwell had shown him set up on top of his desk. Suddenly he was aware that Dallas was not going for his declaration of personal integrity, his rejection of the offer to play ball with the proponents of exploitation. It was as if he had shouted to the heavens that he was righteous, and that the heavens had just laughed back in reply. He was furious.

Buzzing his intercom, he demanded of his secretary an explanation of how the model had gotten there. There was a long pause on the other end.

"Well, Mr. Barnes, the man who brought it said he was from Mr. Maxwell's office . . . he showed me the shipping order . . . said you were expecting it. I just didn't think there would be any problem letting him set it up, seeing that it was from Mr. Maxwell . . . did I do something wrong, Mr. Barnes?"

"No, that's all right, Agnes," Cliff said. No use yelling at the secretary. How should she have known? "Listen, Agnes," he added. "Mr. Maxwell is probably going to ring me up pretty soon. When the call comes in, I advise you to stuff a couple of wads of cotton into your ears so you won't have to hear my obscene screaming. Okay? Oh, and Agnes—"

"Yes, Mr. Barnes?"

"Bring me a cup of coffee, would you?"

He stood there, bent over the model, wondering what had given Maxwell the impression that in spite of his rejection, Cliff Barnes could be bought.

Sue Ellen drove from Cliff's to her mother's in a state of increasing trepidation. How was she going to explain this to Patricia Shepard? That she was going to move in with another man under the very nose of her husband? She did not worry about J.R. or the Ewings. Telling the Ewings would be J.R.'s headache, and he'd just have to live with the truth. Pam, she felt sure, would run straight to J.R. and tell him. Anyway, he was bound to find out sooner or later. But more than J.R.'s wrath, Sue Ellen feared the prospect of her mother's relentless criticism. She had to win her mother over now, or at least get her to accept her decision. It was the only way. But how to do it? She hadn't the vaguest idea. All she could do was pick up her bags and hope that she'd say the right things.

Entering the house, she looked around and didn't see anyone. She ambled into the parlor, taking it all in.

On top of the mantelpiece was a large framed photograph. It had not been there the night before. Sue Ellen went over and held it up to the light. It was her and J.R.'s wedding photograph. She stared at it for a long time, remembering how much in love they'd been. It seemed impossible that everything could have changed as quickly as it did. Their love seemed only a distant memory, making the present state of affairs between them even harder to bear. She suddenly felt like crying, for all the lost years, for all the pain she had been through, for her lost hopes and dreams.

Mrs. Shepard came quietly down the stairs, and mistaking the cause of her daughter's tears, was pleased that her inspiration had had its intended effect. She strode into the parlor, and looking over her daughter's shoulder at the picture of young love, said wistfully, "You two were so beautiful together. I remember how I cried that day . . . tears of happiness, for you and for me. Look how handsome J.R. looked . . . and how happy."

"Those days are gone, Mother, long gone," Sue Ellen whispered through her tears.

"Seven years is not a long time when you stack it up against a lifetime, Sue Ellen," her mother argued.

"It's an eternity when you've spent it married to J.R.," countered her daughter.

Mrs. Shepard walked around the room, staring constantly at Sue Ellen.

"You seem to have done quite well for yourself, from what I can tell," she said.

"I know you believe that, Mother," Sue Ellen responded, overcome with sadness that her mother continued to be blinded by money and power. "Momma," she cried. "Oh, Momma, don't you care that I've been unhappy? Miserable? That I'm withering away out there at Southfork? That I need to have myself back again? Doesn't it matter at all to you how I feel?"

"I've devoted my whole life to you and Kristin," her mother shouted, sounding hurt. "To seeing to it that you were happy, and well provided for! Do you think it pleases me to see you like this? What do you think I am, Sue Ellen? How can you say such a thing to me?"

Sue Ellen shook her head in disbelief. No matter how hard she tried, she did not seem able to get her mother to think of anyone but herself.

Mrs. Shepard, for her part, was still smarting, but there was an element of purpose to her anger, a calculated manipulativeness designed to get her daughter back to her marriage bed. In Mrs. Shepard's world, you did what you had to do to get what you wanted. That's why she liked J.R. so much. He was a man after her own heart.

"Sue Ellen, despite what you're feeling right now, or think you're feeling, married life has more to it than just plain happiness."

"Oh?" said Sue Ellen, perking up her ears. Even she had not expected her mother to go so far as to say something so patently absurd as that. "What else is there, then, Mother?"

"There's security, Sue Ellen, that's what there is. And prestige, and power, and pride, and luxury, and people respecting you, looking up to you! Sue Ellen, if you don't care about any of that, there's nothing I can do to convince you. But at least think of your child! For once in your life, consider somebody else besides yourself!"

"Oh, come off it, Mother!" The voice was that of Kristin, who had descended the stairs in time to hear the tail end of the argument. "You know as well as I do that whether or not Sue Ellen stays with J.R., she'll always have money. Don't you realize what kind of a settlement she can hit him up for? Don't worry about her—she's all taken care of."

Sue Ellen was shocked by her sister's bluntness. Kristin had always been a bit of a brat, but she and Sue Ellen had not seen each other in years, and Sue Ellen had hoped she'd grown out of it. Obviously her little sister had as sharp a tongue as ever, and a mind to go with it.

"There's a difference," Mrs. Shepard was saying, "between being J.R. Ewing's wife and his ex-wife! Several million dollars' difference!"

Sue Ellen had had enough. It was time to leave. "Where are my bags, Mother? I'm moving out of Southfork for good, and I'm suing J.R. for divorce. There's nothing you can say to change my mind, so don't bother trying. It won't do any good."

"You're going back to J.R., young lady," Mrs. Shepard ordered, "and you're going to give him another chance! He may have his faults, but deep down inside he really cares for you! Why, he came here looking for you, didn't he?"

Sue Ellen snorted derisively. "That's only because he's afraid to tell his daddy that his marriage is a failure, and that his baby won't be growing up at Southfork."

"Why don't you just divorce him, then, and get it over with." It was Kristin who spoke, and again her words shocked Sue Ellen. "Well, you don't want him anymore. You said so yourself. And if what you say is true—if he doesn't love you anymore—there isn't any point in staying together, is there? I'll bet you two never really loved each other in the first place—probably just a crush is all."

Sue Ellen was confused. First Kristin had gone to great lengths to praise J.R., and had made it clear that she envied Sue Ellen's good fortune. Now she was agreeing that Sue Ellen should leave him. What was on her mind?

What was on Kristin's mind was marriage. If Sue Ellen did not want J.R., she knew someone who did. After all, what was the harm in moving in on somebody else's abandoned marriage? With Sue Ellen out of the picture, J.R. would be Dallas's most eligible bachelor. And Kristin could not help but feel that she had a very long and shapely leg up on the competition.

"Where are you going to go now?" Mrs. Shepard asked, moving on to other considerations. "Stay here with us, Sue Ellen. You belong with your family! Why, didn't we come here all the way from Boca Raton just to be with you and the baby?"

Kristin laughed at her mother's hypocrisy. "We came to Dallas to find me a rich husband, Momma. No need to lie about that; there's nothing wrong with it."

Sue Ellen marveled at how much brighter her little sister was than she herself had been at that age. So much brighter, and more soulless. She thought of herself at nineteen, when she had married J.R. How she had loved him! It was heaven, being in love with a fabulously wealthy and powerful man. She had continued to love him for a long time, tying her every goal to his, always thinking that she could change his little bad points. But the bad points had grown bigger and bigger, and Sue Ellen, thinking that if she never complained, never argued, if she kept on being the perfect wife to him, she could somehow make him love her! She knew more and more that she was not what he wanted and yet kept on trying to make herself fit his expectations. It had been a joke. Just a bad, impossible joke. But the joke was over now.

"If I believed for a moment that he could ever love me again the way he used to in the beginning, I would go back, even now. But that will never happen, Momma . . . never . . . never . . . never . . ."

Sue Ellen dissolved into bitter tears. Even Mrs. Shepard was moved by the sight of her daughter's grief, and took her tenderly in her arms, rocking and comforting her.

Kristin stood watching the pitiful scene, a serene smile on her face, making plans of her own.

The intercom finally buzzed on Cliff Barnes' desk, and he readied himself for Ben Maxwell's phone call. But it wasn't a phone call, and it wasn't Maxwell. His secretary informed him that J.R. Ewing was in the outer office, waiting to see him.

Cliff found himself totally caught off guard. He feared at once that J.R. had found out about him and Sue Ellen—what other possible reason could he have had to come calling in person on his most hated enemy?

Cliff had vaguely thought about this eventuality ever since he and Sue Ellen had started seeing each other, but after a while, when they had been together for a couple of months and nothing had happened, he had gotten the notion, way back in his head, that maybe nothing *would* happen, maybe J.R. would never find out. However, it should have occurred to him that once Sue Ellen moved in with him, it would all be out in the open and he would have to deal with it.

He had managed to avoid thinking about it altogether, but now reality had reared its ugly head and he had very little time to think. He told Agnes to stall the visitor for a moment. He paced the room, straightened his clothes, took a deep breath and asked her to show J.R. in.

J.R. was thinking about the time, only a few weeks ago, when he had had Cliff Barnes lined up in the cross hairs of his rifle sight, and could have blown him off the face of the earth. It would have been called an accident. After all, the whole idea was to free Bobby from kidnappers. Barnes had accused him of attempting to murder him. How ironic, J.R. thought.

"I don't know why I didn't blow your brains out when I had the chance," he said as he entered Cliff's office.

"Maybe you only have murder in your mind, not in your trigger finger," said Cliff.

J.R. laughed. "You're just lucky I didn't know

then what I know now." He checked to see if Cliff was going to pretend innocence but could see that he was not. "What a tawdry little fling you two have had." He shook his head in disgust. "Tawdry, that's what it was . . . you're a tawdry little person, Barnes, with tawdry hopes and dreams. All you want is revenge on us Ewings for the way we treated your daddy. Your problem, as I see it, is that tawdry men like you are no match for elegant, high-class, expensive sluts like Sue Ellen. She'd have bankrupted you in no time."

Cliff shook his head slowly. Once again, J.R. was showing where his heart lay. All he ever cared about was money.

"How much are you offering me to get out of her life, J.R.?" Cliff spat out.

J.R. laughed, a great whooping belly laugh. He seemed genuinely amused.

"How much? How much? I don't know if you've got a sense of humor or if you're just plain stupid—I'm not gonna offer you a thing, Barnes. I'm just inviting you to call off this little affair of yours, and I'm advising you to accept my invitation."

Cliff stood up, his anger visible on his features. All his hatred of the Ewings, and of J.R. in particular, was ammunition for his defense.

"I'm not getting out, J.R. Sue Ellen is going to be the mother of my child . . . *my* child . . . and I'm the one who's gonna raise it and be a father to it!"

"That's a charming little fairy tale you just

made up, Barnes." J.R. smiled, sitting on the edge of Cliff's desk, and spinning his cowboy hat in his hands. "I suppose it's possible that the child is yours . . . might be anybody's, for that matter . . . even mine . . . but that child, no matter who the father is, is going to be mine. It's going to be a Ewing, and live at Southfork, and be the heir to Ewing Oil and a great fortune. And I'm gonna be its daddy. 'Cause that child's gonna be too big for a little man like you to raise."

Fear clutched Cliff in the throat as he listened to J.R. He knew he hadn't the resources to challenge him. Nevertheless, in this life, one had to stand up for what one believed in.

"J.R.," he said, coming right up to his adversary, "I advise you not to try and get in the way of Sue Ellen and me. It would be mighty troublesome for you. Think about it . . . if this all came out in court, and on the front pages of the papers, how would you explain it all to your daddy and your momma? How are you going to tell them that your wife's baby was fathered by Cliff Barnes?"

J.R. did not even blink. He had thought this out beforehand and knew exactly what to say.

"Yes," he admitted, "that would be awful for me, no doubt about it. It would be very painful . . . but, after a time, my daddy and momma, and everyone else in Dallas, for that matter, would come to the opinion that it was all the fault of the loose woman I had the bad judgment to marry. 'Poor J.R.,' they'll say, 'what a scandal! Lifted a woman up out of the gutter, only to have her fall right back into it! And with Cliff Barnes! How low can a person fall!' Sloppy seconds, Cliff, that's what you'd be left with."

Cliff stormed to the door and opened it wide.

"Get out of my sight!" he ordered.

But J.R. did not even move.

"Close that door, Cliff, and come back here. I'm not through talking," he said. "What I was about to say, before I was so rudely interrupted, was that yes, it would be bad for me, and it'd be worse for Sue Ellen, but the person who'd really be slitting his throat is you."

He paused for a moment to let this sink in, noticing Cliff's puzzled face. The fight seemed to have gone out of him instantly, replaced by the fear that had been lurking just below the surface.

"Look at it this way, Barnes. I am a successful man, and the reason for that is that I know how to beat the other guy at his own game. I've known you for years, Cliff. I know what you're after. You want to be powerful—so powerful that you can destroy us Ewings. That's going to take a lot of power . . . maybe governor or senator before you're really able to hurt us. Your problem is, a man tainted with scandal can't get elected garbageman. You should have learned that in the last election.

"You know, you really are at a disadvantage, being poor and relatively unconnected. For me, all doors are open. If I wanted to be governor, I probably could swing it all by myself, with a little help from friends. Even scandal couldn't hurt me. When you're a multimillionaire oilman, people expect that sort of behavior from you. But those same people demand a lot more of their garden-variety elected officials. If I ever took you and Sue Ellen to court and dragged the whole thing out into the open, I'd embarrass myself, but your career would be over. Forever."

Cliff felt his bravado disintegrate within seconds. J.R. was putting it plainly. It was either give up Sue Ellen, or give up everything else he wanted in life.

"You wouldn't," he said weakly.

"You're not giving me any other option, as I see it," said J.R. in his most businesslike tone. "Sue Ellen's going to be calling you soon, I believe. You'd better make up your mind so you'll know what to say to her."

"What do you expect me to say?" asked Cliff.

"Oh, the whole truth and nothing but the truth." J.R. smiled, putting on his hat and making for the door. "Tell her that you love her, but you love something else more." And with that, he was gone.

Cliff stared after him for a long time. Then his gaze fell on the model. Suddenly, violently, he swept the buildings onto the floor with one swipe of his hand, unable to bear the taunting of the model's promise.

When J.R. rang Mrs. Shepard's door this time, she was not in the least surprised. In fact, she had been expecting him for quite some time, knowing that by now he must have a lead on Sue Ellen's whereabouts. She welcomed him sympathetically, but he was not in the mood for sympathy. He had murder in his eyes, and he was all business.

"Where's Sue Ellen?" he asked evenly.

"I'll get her," said Mrs. Shepard. But she could not resist saying, "I'm so sorry things have come to this, J.R. You know how much I want things to work out between you."

"Thank you, Patricia," he said softly. "Don't worry. I feel that if Sue Ellen will just listen to what I have to say, everything will be all right."

"Is there any way I can help, J.R.?"

"Thank you again, Patricia, but no. It's good to know I can count on you, but I think I can handle this one myself."

Finally, she headed upstairs to fetch Sue Ellen.

J.R. went into the living room, looking around. His eyes fell on the wedding photo, and he couldn't suppress a grim, pained little smile. He turned as he heard his wife enter the room.

"What is it, J.R.? I understand you have something to say to me."

"Well, darlin'," he said apologetically, "I came to see if I could convince you to come home with me."

She laughed, tossing her hair out of her eyes, which were bright and flashing with anger.

"I see," she said. "You miss me terribly and you're brokenhearted about my leaving, is that it?"

"You don't have to be sarcastic, Sue Ellen. You know why I want you home."

"That's right," she agreed. "I do know why, and that's the very reason I'm never coming back to Southfork."

"I'm even ready to forgive your little peccadillo with Cliff Barnes."

He watched as she started, taken aback that he had found out so easily. But almost as quickly as the shock had overtaken her, she regained her former state of resolve.

"I see. Isn't it wonderful to have a staff of paid detectives to spy on people for you. So you know about me and Cliff. And you're willing to be magnanimous. Well, I'm not willing to forgive the hundreds of times you've cheated on me! If anything drove me into Cliff Barnes' arms, it was you! I'm not taking orders from you anymore, J.R. Not ever."

J.R. moved closer to her, so that his face was only inches from hers.

"Oh, yes you will, darlin'," he growled. "You have no choice. I'm prepared, if you force me into it, to take drastic action. There are hospitals that take care of problems like yours. If that baby isn't going to be raised at Southfork, it isn't going to be raised at all. The papers will say you had a tragic miscarriage, and then there'll be a scandalous divorce proceeding. You'll be broke, childless, and you won't even have the Ewing name to trade on."

Sue Ellen was speechless, knocked for a loop by her husband's incredible threat. She could not believe that even J.R. would stoop to something like that, but the tone in his voice was deadly serious and she could not be sure that he wouldn't.

"You wouldn't ever do that, J.R.," she said, her voice shaking. "Cliff wouldn't let you get away with it."

Now J.R. laughed scornfully and moved away from her again.

"Oh, is that right? Okay, Sue Ellen . . . I'll be fair about this. Give old Cliff a call right now and ask him how far he'll go for you. Better yet, go over and see him. I think you'll find you can't count on him in the crunch. Go ahead . . . ask him."

Sue Ellen was shaking violently now, out of control. How could J.R. be so sure that Cliff would not help her? She could not believe that Cliff would abandon her in a crisis, and yet J.R. had seemed so sure of what he was saying. She quickly spun around and ran out the door.

She had to know, and she had to know right away. Her life was falling down all around her, the walls of her rebellion collapsing, and Cliff was the only hope she had left.

After the door had slammed behind her, J.R. straightened his tie. He turned around just in time to see Mrs. Shepard and Kristin coming down the stairs. How discreet of them, he thought, amused, to pretend that they had not heard every word.

"Ladies . . ." he greeted them with a smile. "I think Sue Ellen is about to come to her senses."

"Great," replied Kristin, but her disappointment was evident in her tone.

Mrs. Shepard, on the other hand, was genuinely pleased. "Isn't that wonderful! Oh, I'm so relieved."

J.R. knew what they were waiting for next. "Say, Patricia, now that all this is over, I think it'd be nice if you came out to Southfork, spent a lot of time with Sue Ellen. I think it'd be good for her to see a lot of her momma."

The smile on Mrs. Shepard's face could have lit up Times Square.

"Why, of course, J.R. Anything to help Sue Ellen . . ." she gushed.

Kristin was eyeing J.R., trying to figure him out. There was something underneath it all, some mystery about the man that made him very attractive to her.

"And Kristin, that goes for you as well. I'd like for you to spend a lot of time at the ranch . . . a *lot* of time."

From his look, which had no mystery about it at all, Kristin knew she would be doing just that.

Sue Ellen felt as if she were drowning. She drove to Cliff's house at a dangerous pace, and when she got there and looked into his eyes, she knew that J.R. had been there before her. She suggested that they go to the park, to "their place" —the path they had walked so often when their love affair had been new. Silently, they got into the car.

As they walked, Sue Ellen told Cliff about J.R.'s threat and about his suggestion that she ask Cliff for help. There was pain in Cliff's eyes as she spoke, and she could sense that he had already withdrawn from her. Still, she could not quite believe that it was all over. She refused to believe it until she heard it from his own lips.

But all Cliff could do was shrug. "It's too much for me, Sue Ellen . . . the odds are too great against us. We'd both be destroyed in the end."

She could not believe it! "Don't you love me, Cliff? You said you did . . ."

"Yes," he agreed, "and I do . . . as much as I can love any person. But what J.R. showed me, and he was right, is that there are things I need more than the love of a woman, and he's making me choose between those things . . . and you."

Her heart twisted into a painful knot. "Oh, Cliff . . ." she whispered tearfully, "what would be so terrible about being just the two of us, without all the trappings?"

"I need those 'trappings,' as you call them, Sue Ellen. They're what I've worked for all my life. I'd never forgive you—or myself—for giving them up. Not even for love . . ."

"You're not the only one who'd be giving up a lot for the relationship, you know." Suddenly she felt used, victimized. Here she had been willing to give up everything, and Cliff was not willing to give up much at all.

"J.R. said it better than I could explain it to you," he said. "See, he told me that the reason he's successful is that he beats the other guy at his own game. That's what he did with us. You and I are going to have to learn to do that, too.

We're going to have to learn J.R.'s game and beat him at it."

Again, Sue Ellen was stung by his words. So it was all a game between him and J.R., and she had been only a pawn. J.R. had captured her, and so the game was over, and she was the prize.

"Cliff," she whispered, "it's over. I'm so sorry it turned out this way . . . so sorry you turned out to be the person you did . . . so sorry for all of us." She could speak no more. Without another word, or even a wave of the hand, she turned and swiftly walked away.

Behind her, Cliff crouched on the ground and buried his head in his hands, his emotions battered and bruised, unable to speak or even to move.

As Sue Ellen reached her car and made to open the door, the door of the car next to hers opened, and from the driver's seat J.R. called to her to get inside. "I'll have one of the boys come by for your car," he said. "Your mother was kind enough to pack your things and put them in the back."

He waited for her to get in, and knowing she had no choice, no mind of her own any longer, she got in, silently, slowly, sitting beside him in stony silence.

"Well," he said cheerfully, as though nothing had happened, "tonight the whole family will be at dinner. It'll be just like old times. You'll tell them all about your nice restful stay with your momma. Yeah, it'll be just the same as before.

Just like old times." He started the car and pulled out into the traffic. "Oh, and while I have it in mind, I'll be going out after dinner. I have a late business meeting in town. Don't stay up all night waiting—this one could take a while."

She looked at him. His meaning was clear, and this time there was no fighting with him. She sighed in resignation and looked helplessly out of the window. For now, the victory was his. But soon . . . soon . . . she would find a way to be free. And then he would never bully her again. Never.

Back in his office once more, Cliff, too, was feeling battered and angry. Never again, he swore to himself, would J.R. Ewing push him around. Whatever it took, he was going to see to it that from now on he had the power to fight back. He looked around the room at the smashed, scattered model buildings and bent over to pick them up and put them back into place. Resolve was replacing resignation, and when he was through cleaning up, he went over to the phone and dialed Ben Maxwell.

"Ben?" he said, determination and anger mixing in his voice, "Cliff Barnes here. You've got yourself a deal. That development is as good as built, and on top of that, any other development you want is yours, too. You just get me the power, and I'll do whatever you say. The more power, the more you get in return." He listened as Maxwell agreed, and then hung up the phone, his appointment as head of the Office of Land Management assured.

"Now, J.R. Ewing," he said softly, "now we shall see who can beat whom at the other man's game!"